No Escape from Love

Barbara Cartland

No Escape from Love

DURON BOOKS

No Escape from Love
A Duron Book / November 1977

Library of Congress Cataloging in Publication Data

Cartland, Barbara, 1902–
No escape from love.
I. Title.
PZ3.C247Nk   1977   [PR6005.A765]   823'.9'12   77–21225
ISBN 0–87272–029–2

Duron Books are published by Brodart, Inc., Williamsport, Pa. Its trademark, consisting of the words "Duron Books" is registered in the United States Patent Office and in other countries.

PRINTED IN THE UNITED STATES OF AMERICA

No Escape from Love

Chapter One

1805

"It is finished, Mama."

Lady Waltham, who had been lying back against her pillows with her eyes closed, opened them and said softly:

"I am so glad, darling."

Her voice was very weak, and although she was abnormally thin, almost to the point of emaciation, and so pale that her skin looked translucent, it was still possible to realise that she had been a very beautiful woman.

Her daughter, Vernita, was also thin but she had the grace and beauty of youth, and now she stood up and held up a négligée for her mother's inspection.

Of Indian muslin with open-work embroidery, the gown was bordered with pale rose muslin and fastened with bows of the same material, while the trimmings were of point lace.

It seemed curiously out of place in the bare attic room with its wooden floors and uncurtained windows.

"You have made it beautifully, dearest," Lady Waltham said, "and let us hope they will pay you at once."

"I have been thinking, Mama," Vernita said, "that

1

I will not take it to Maison Claré but direct to the
Princess Borghese herself."

"You cannot do that," Lady Waltham said, her
voice a little stronger as she spoke in protest. "It
would be dangerous. Besides, it was Maison Claré
which ordered it."

"They cheat us," Vernita replied. "They give us
a mere pittance for everything we make and charge
their customers exorbitant sums."

"We should starve without them," Lady Waltham
pointed out.

"We shall starve anyway if we do not obtain
more money for our sewing," Vernita replied.

She spoke in the plural although in fact it was
only she who had been able to sew in the last few
months.

Lady Waltham had grown weaker and weaker
but they did not dare to send for a Doctor, and Vernita knew it was not medical attention which her
mother needed but food.

It was in fact incredible that they had managed
to survive for so long while living in hiding, and,
having sold everything of any value they possessed,
they had been forced to rely on what they could
make with their fingers.

It was two years ago, Vernita thought, that they
had first come to Paris with her father, as had thou-
sands of other English visitors, when the Treaty of
Amiens had put an end to the years of hostility between France and England.

The summer of 1802 had seen England relaxing
in the sunshine of the Amiens agreement.

Worn out by nine years of strife, crushing tax-
ation, and starvation-causing prices, everyone re-
joiced at the return of peace and plenty.

Once the fighting was finished, the good-humoured British ceased to worry about Napoleon
Bonaparte, the young conqueror of Austria and Italy,
and even accepted his control of the Dutch Coast.

Tourists who had endured the years of enmity
and who longed for the delights of foreign travel

flooded across the Channel, and the ports on both sides were crowded with rank and fashion.

Sir Edward Waltham had prudently waited until the first rush and excitement had abated, and it was not until the following year, in March 1803, that with his wife and daughter Vernita he set off for Paris.

They had found the city as attractive as Vernita had expected and were entertained by a great number of friends and acquaintances.

They had seen the First Consul Napoleon Bonaparte at a Diplomatic Reception and thought him an attractive, almost handsome man, very unlike the cartoons in which he had been depicted as a villainous monster.

It was therefore all the more of a shock when in May, as they were looking forward to a summer of levees, Assemblies, and Balls, the Armistice came to an end.

Napoleon Bonaparte was furious.

The war he had intended had come, but too soon! By forcing the issue before his Navy was ready, the English had regained half the ground they had lost in the Amiens peace treaty.

But the English who were abroad were not aware of what their Government was doing and ten thousand British tourists were arrested and interned.

Such an action entailing the imprisonment of civilians was contrary to all civilised precedents, and the British at home were appalled and convinced more than ever that they were dealing with an untamed savage.

This, however, was no consolation for those who found themselves dragged from the houses where they were staying or the elegant Hôtels they had rented for the Season.

It was only because Sir Edward had a friend in the French Government that he had been warned of what was to happen twelve hours before the edict was put into operation.

Hurriedly he left with his wife and daughter for a house in a small, unfashionable back-street which let rooms to anyone who enquired for them and whose proprietor asked no questions.

Unfortunately, while Sir Edward was planning how they could get home to England—although it seemed likely to be impossible—he was taken ill.

Vernita was convinced that it was the water of Paris that was responsible for his illness.

But, whatever it was, they had no sooner reached the sanctuary of their boarding house than Sir Edward began to run a high temperature.

Although his wife and daughter tended him in every way they could, he died suddenly after a week's agonising pain, leaving them stunned, helpless, and alone.

Too late they realised that they should have risked disclosure and sent for a Doctor.

Even so, the medical service in France had a bad name and it was doubtful that even the most experienced Physician could have saved Sir Edward.

Lady Waltham, who had loved her husband dearly, was prostrated with grief, and it was Vernita who arranged that they should move from the more comfortable apartments they occupied up into the attic.

Sir Edward had quite a considerable sum of ready cash on him, since as soon as he had learnt that they must go into hiding he had drawn out the full amount of his Letters of Credit from the Bank.

But Vernita sensibly realised that this would not last forever; and as the war before the Armistice had lasted for nine years, she thought with a sinking of her heart that now that hostilities had resumed they might continue for another nine.

"We must save every possible penny," she said to Lady Waltham.

She realised from her mother's helpless response that it was up to her to take the lead and play her father's part in deciding everything they should do.

It was obvious that Napoleon's wrath against the British was echoed by all Frenchmen.

Vernita learnt that the Corsican's craving for revenge had made him intent on conquering the race of "insolent shop-keepers" who barred his way to world domination.

The newspapers reported that he was determined to cross the Channel and invade England.

"They want us to jump the ditch," he cried, "and we will jump it!"

He ordered the construction of hundreds of invasion barges and gun-boats to carry an Army to England and mobilised every French sea-port.

The French thrilled to his vision and jeered at the British who thought they could defend themselves against such an Armada.

However, time passed and by the beginning of 1805 Napoleon began to realise that his dream of crossing the Channel was fading while the British Navy blocked the way. But that was not to say that Paris was any more tolerant towards the English.

Every time Vernita went out shopping or walked along the streets she could almost feel the hatred for her countrymen emanating from the "Victorious French," who had the rest of Europe under their heels.

But victories did not stop the price of food from rising and Vernita was finding it more and more difficult to feed herself and her mother.

Lady Waltham had never recovered from the shock of her husband's death and she seemed to her daughter to be fading away, month after month, day after day.

Yet there was nothing Vernita could do about it except give themselves up to the authorities.

Every nerve in her body shrank from the thought of internment, and something resolute and proud within her made her determined to go on fighting, even if she died in the effort.

Now, looking at her mother in the spring sunshine, she knew that something had to be done and done quickly.

It was while she was sitting completing the elegant négligée she had made on the orders of the

Maison Claré that she decided she would take it
directly to the customer who had ordered it.

She was well aware that Princess Paulina Borghese had bought a great number of beautiful garments which her mother and she had made so
painstakingly.

Even when the Princess had been in Italy last
year, orders had come back to Paris for chemises,
nightgowns, and négligées which had to be made in
record time so that they could be carried by Courier
to Rome.

The Maison Claré imposed sweated labour upon
their seamstresses.

When Vernita called at the shop to collect materials and laces that she was to fashion into the
elegant garments for their customers, she had realised how high their prices were and how much
those who made them were exploited.

She felt herself resenting the fact that while she
and her mother were employed almost exclusively on
garments made at break-neck speed for the Princess,
the Maison Claré would not pay them any more.

The Coronation which had taken place last December had increased the demand for lingerie as
beautiful and ornate as the gowns that were to be
worn over it.

Orders from Princess Paulina poured in, and
when Vernita protested that it was impossible for
them to do all that was expected in so short a time,
she was told abruptly to do as she was told or she
would be dismissed and they would find someone
else.

That, she thought, was unlikely, but she dared
not risk open defiance.

Only now, when she had finished the muslin
négligée, which was more elaborate and indeed more
beautiful than anything the Princess had bought before, did she decide to take matters into her own
hands.

"I will wear Louise's best gown and hat, Mama,"
she said, "and I will look the typical *petite bourgeoise*

and no-one will suspect for a moment that I am any-thing else."

"It is too much of a risk," Lady Waltham said feebly. "Suppose it is discovered who you are?"

"Then we will go to prison," Vernita said, "and perhaps we will be better off. At least they feed the prisoners."

Lady Waltham gave a little cry and her daughter went to her side.

"I am only teasing, Mama. No-one will guess for a moment that I am not what I appear to be. After all, when I go shopping, the shop-keepers are just as rude to me as they are to all the other poor women who stand hesitating as they choose the cheapest cabbage and haggle over every *sou.*"

"If only this terrible war were over," Lady Wal-tham said, "or we had never come to Paris."

There was a sob in her voice which told Vernita that she was thinking of her husband and wishing they had never left their home in England.

'It is all my fault,' Vernita thought, as she had done so often before.

Because her father had decided that at seven-teen she should have the benefit of foreign travel, they had set out from their Manor House in Bucking-hamshire, which had been in the Waltham family for five generations.

She felt a sharp pang of misery and regret that fortune should have treated them so harshly. Then with a philosophical smile she told herself, in the words of her old Nanny, that it was "no use crying over spilt milk."

She and her mother were here in Paris, and there was nothing they could do about it except try to survive.

She bent down and kissed Lady Waltham's cold cheek.

"I am going downstairs to find Louise," she said. "She is kind and I know she will not refuse to help me."

Lady Waltham did not protest, knowing that if

Vernita was set on doing something, nothing would dissuade her from the path she had chosen.

At the same time, she could not help thinking how cruel it was that her daughter, who was so pretty and so attractive, must spend her life sewing against time in this miserable, poverty-stricken attic.

At home she would be entertaining the County, riding her horses over her father's estate, and attending Balls and Assemblies in London to which she would automatically be invited by the *Beau Monde*.

"What will happen to her in the future?" Lady Waltham wondered miserably.

She thought that, even whilst she had prayed and prayed that Vernita might be saved from the terrible life they were leading there had been no answer and even God seemed to have deserted her now.

"Oh, Edward!" she said speaking aloud to her husband as she often did when she was alone, "wherever you are, surely you can help us?"

Because she was so weak the thought of her husband brought the tears to Lady Waltham's eyes.

Then as she heard the sound of Vernita coming up the uncarpeted stairs she wiped them away, knowing it upset her daughter to see her cry.

Vernita came into the room carrying a black gown over her arm and a small black straw hat in her hand.

"Louise has been most kind, as I knew she would be," she said, "but I must be very careful with these hideous garments because they are her Sunday best! Now watch me, Mama, transform myself into exactly the kind of seamstress Her Imperial Highness would expect to find working on her lingerie."

Usually when Vernita went out into the street she wore a shawl over her head and a shapeless coat which disguised her slender figure.

This was not only to avoid being suspected of being a foreigner but also to keep amorous young Frenchmen from noticing the huge violet-coloured eyes which seemed almost too big for her lovely face.

When she was dressed in Louise's black gown,

which reached high at the neck and down to her wrists, she looked a typical *petite bourgeoise* and at the same time a very attractive one.

Lady Waltham looked at her almost in horror.

"You cannot go out like that, dearest! A man might speak to you. You might be insulted!"

"I am only going to the Rue du Faubourg Saint Honoré, Mama, and I will keep to the side-streets and avoid the Boulevards. No-one will speak to me, I promise you."

"I hope not," Lady Waltham said nervously, "but really, dearest, that ridiculous hat is quite becoming."

"You are prejudiced, Mama," Vernita replied, "and I promise you I shall be quite safe."

She packed up the négligée, then looked round the room to see if there was anything her mother wanted.

"Do not worry if I am a little longer than you expect," she said. "When I get the money for this I shall buy milk on my way home, and perhaps if I receive as much as I hope—a chicken!"

"You must not be extravagant," Lady Waltham said almost automatically.

"Are we ever that?" Vernita asked with a touch of bitterness in her voice.

She kissed her mother tenderly.

"At least the sunshine is warm today," she said, "but, darling Mama, do not leave your hands outside the sheets. You know how cold they get."

As she spoke she thought how severe the winter had been and how desperately cold both she and her mother became during the long dark nights when they could not afford heating of any sort.

Sometimes Vernita thought they would both be found stiff and dead in the morning.

But by a miracle they had survived, although at times she had awoken in the night, tense and fearful, to listen and reassure herself that her mother was still breathing.

Now as she hurried down the stairs towards the front door she felt it would be a relief to get out into the fresh air and clear away her headache, which she knew came from sewing for so long and having so little food.

The house in which they lived had better-off tenants on the first and second floors, and the Concierge and his wife, *Monsieur* and *Madame* Danjou, who were in charge of the building, were in consequence tolerant towards the poverty-striken mother and daughter who lived in the top attic.

If they were suspicious that the Walthams were not all they appeared to be they certainly gave no indication of it either to Lady Waltham or to Vernita.

They knew them, of course, as *Madame* and *Mademoiselle* Bernier, which was the name Sir Edward had chosen when they went into hiding, saying it was as ordinary and commonplace as Smith, Jones, or Brown would be in England.

Monsieur and *Madame* Danjou had one daughter, Louise, who was about the same age as Vernita.

Louise because she liked Vernita was always suggesting that they should go out together in the evening and perhaps find someone who would accompany them to the cheap places of amusement where the young people of Paris congregated.

She could not understand why Vernita always refused, her excuse being that she could not leave her mother.

"You are wasting your youth," Louise said more than once with a note of scorn in her voice. "If you are not careful, *M'mselle,* you will *coiffer* Saint Catherine."

This meant that Vernita would become an old maid.

But while Vernita would laugh at the idea when she was talking to Louise, she sometimes wondered herself if she would ever know any other life but the confines of the cold, uncomfortable attic and the companionship of her mother.

She missed the young people of her own age whom she had known at home in England. She missed too the conversations she had enjoyed with her father and the books they had read together.

Sir Edward had been a very intelligent man and he had had his daughter well educated, with the result that now that she was bound in by poverty and fear, Vernita felt sometimes that her brain was turning to sawdust and that she had ceased to think of anything but money.

"Mama must have some food, and quickly," she told herself now as she walked towards the Rue du Faubourg Saint Honoré.

She took as she had promised the empty side-streets and avoided the busy Boulevards with their traffic and perambulating crowds moving along the pavements or sitting outside the Cafés.

Finally she found herself in the right road, and without much difficulty, because she had seen it in the past, identified the Hôtel de Charost, the magnificent Mansion which now belonged to Her Imperial Highness Princess Paulina Borghese.

Napoleon had at his Coronation as Emperor elevated his brothers Joseph and Louis to the rank of Princes. His sisters were however furious at the idea of their brother's wives being Princesses but not themselves.

They made such a scene that Napoleon had said wryly:

"To hear my sisters talk, anyone would think I had defrauded them of their rightful heritage from our late father, the King."

However, after tears and reproaches he gave way and announced that in the future "the sisters of the Emperor would bear the title of Imperial Highness."

The entrance to the Hôtel de Charost was very impressive and the black marble plaque surmounted with heraldry over the lofty gateway proclaimed that its erstwhile owners had been far more aristocratic than its present occupant.

Passing through the gateway, Vernita found herself in a courtyard, the walls on either side curving in a semi-circle.

Now she felt nervous, fearing that she would be

turned away and that after all she would have to take
what she had made to the Maison Claré and accept
the pittance they were prepared to give her for it.

"What is your business?" a flunkey asked in a
harsh voice, not particularly impressed by her appearance.

His livery was green and Vernita had heard that
it was the Princess's favourite colour.

"I have brought the négligée for Her Imperial
Highness that she ordered."

She was half-afraid the flunkey would take it
from her and she would not have the chance, as she
had hoped, of soliciting further orders, but instead he
motioned her to enter the front door and she found
herself in a Hall with marble columns and painted
panels.

There was a staircase of steel and gilt with a
sweep which showed a ramp decorated with sun-
heads and lilies.

Not that Vernita had much time to look around
her. She was led into a room where the Princess was
already in discussion with several people whose
trade was dressmaking and millinery.

The Princess, wearing a diaphanous green
déshabillé which did little to conceal the exquisite
lines of her Grecian figure, was half-lying on a chaise
longue while materials for a new gown were being
offered for her approval.

Vernita had learnt from the Maison Claré that
the Princess much preferred the smaller fashion-house
of La Petite Leblanc to the more famous and fashionable dressmaker Leroy.

This morning, however, it appeared that neither
the material nor the design pleased her.

"It is not chic," she was saying imperiously as
Vernita entered the room. "In fact I should look
hideous in that, so you can take it away and design
something better."

"Mais, Madame . . ." the designer began, only to
be interrupted.

"*Pardi!* I cannot believe you intend to argue with me!"

The Princess spoke with a sudden flashing anger which was completely in contrast to her appearance, which made her seem light as thistledown and lovelier than any Grecian statue.

The newspapers had always described her as representing the ideal of classical beauty, but Vernita had not realised that she was in fact far more beautiful than any words in which they had extolled her.

Her features were perfect; her face was so lovely that it seemed almost incongruous that she should be annoyed by anything or anybody.

Then as the dressmaker turned to leave, she smiled an amused, tantalising smile at a gentleman seated in an arm-chair beside her.

It transformed her face and curved her lips with an entrancing provocation that was indescribably attractive.

It was difficult for Vernita to take her eyes from anything so lovely, but as the Princess beckoned to the next applicant for her favours, a woman with two bonnet-cases on her arm, she glanced at the gentleman in the arm-chair.

He too looked as if he had stepped out of a story-book. He was slim and elegant and was sitting back at his ease with his legs crossed.

There was a slightly cynical expression in his eyes and a twist to his mouth as if he was contemptuous of the whole proceeding.

He would be tall when he was standing, Vernita decided, and he had broad shoulders and an authoritative air about him which made her think of her father.

She thought, although she was not sure, that he was not very young, definitely over thirty, and she wondered who he was.

Then as the Princess smiled at him again Vernita was certain what his position was in the household.

The Princess's amatory indiscretions had been

written up in the newspapers with a frankness that left little to the imagination.

It was well-known too that her brother Napoleon Bonaparte had, as soon as she was widowed on her husband's death in battle, hurried to find her another husband who would keep her in order.

She had been married for two years to the Prince Camillo Borghese, and at the time their engagement was announced, Sir Edward Waltham had remarked it was a splendid match for a girl coming from an unimportant Corsican family to marry one of the greatest and noblest of Italian aristocrats.

Because at seventeen Vernita was romantic, she had, when she first came to Paris, learnt all she could about Prince Camillo Borghese.

She learnt that he was twenty-eight and a handsome Roman with dark, curling hair and shining, dark eyes.

He was incredibly wealthy, owning vast estates in Italy, and had a most impressive roll of titles.

Her mother had shared her interest in the match and had said to Vernita:

"The Borghese family jewels are said to be the finest in the world and their treasures are one of the best private collections ever known."

The Prince and Princess had been engaged before the Armistice had come to an end and married the following August.

All Paris had been in a state of excitement about the wedding and Vernita had learnt of it through *Madame* Danjou and Louise.

It was only later that year that Vernita, when seeking work to replenish their tiny capital which was gradually vanishing, had learnt from the Maison Claré that the lingerie she was making would be worn by the Princess in whom she had been so interested.

One thing she knew quite clearly was that the gentleman at whom the Princess was now smiling so invitingly was not her husband, and now as the mil-

liner displayed an attractive bonnet trimmed with
green ostrich-feathers he said to the Princess:

"I think that would suit you."

"Are you sure?" the Princess enquired. "I thought
perhaps the brim was a little too high."

"It will frame your lovely face like a halo."

"Do you think I deserve one?"

She looked at him from under her eye-lashes in a
provocative manner.

"I think you *need* one," he answered, and she
laughed, showing her perfect teeth as she did so.

Then as if he had made up her mind for her the
Princess said:

"All right, I will take it. Bring some more tomorrow. Something new, something I have not worn already."

"*Merci bien, Madame la Princesse!*" the milliner
said, bowing to the floor.

Now the Princess looked at Vernita for the first
time.

She made a little sign with her hand, and with
her heart beating rapidly Vernita moved forward to
curtsey in front of the *chaise longue.*

"Who are you? I have not seen you before!" the
Princess enquired.

"I have brought the négligée you ordered, *Madame la Princesse,*" Vernita said.

She thought the Princess looked puzzled and
quickly she undid the parcel and took out the négligée, shaking it clear of the paper and holding it
up so that the Princess could see how captivating
it was with its frills and open-work embroidery.

"*Mais oui!*" the Princess exclaimed. "It is en-
chanting! It will suit me just as I thought it would!"

She rose as she spoke from the *chaise longue*
and, to Vernita's astonishment, started to pull off the
green négligée she wore and the nightgown that was
underneath it.

She flung them down on the floor and stood there
naked, more beautiful than any sculptured goddess

could possibly have been, perfect from the top of her head to her delicate little feet.

Blushing crimson from embarrassment that any woman, especially a Princess, should behave in such a way in front of a gentleman, Vernita quickly helped her into the robe.

The Princess fastened it and turned towards the gentleman, who was watching her, holding out her arms and pirouetting round so that he could see her from every angle.

"What do you think, Axel?" she asked. "Tell me how I look."

"As lovely as an angel," he answered.

"Thank you." She smiled. "That is what I wanted you to say."

She turned to Vernita.

"You tell me that you made this?"

"*Oui, Madame la Princesse*, I made it, as I have made all the lingerie you have ordered recently."

Vernita paused for a moment. Then as she realised the Princess was still listening she said:

"But Maison Claré pays me very little—so little, in fact, that I have come directly to you because I would like, *Madame la Princesse,* to continue to make such beautiful things for Your Imperial Highness but I cannot afford to do so unless I can obtain more money for them."

Her heart was thumping as she spoke, and her hands trembled.

Would this lovely but immodest woman, she wondered, ever understand what it meant to work as hard as she and her mother had worked this past year and know that every *sou* made the difference between being just hungry and being ravenous?

"What does Maison Claré pay you?"

It was not the Princess who spoke but the gentleman she had called Axel.

Remembering who she was supposed to be, Vernita curtseyed to him before she answered; and because she somehow felt he was sympathetic she told him quickly what she had been paid for a négligée, a nightgown, and a chemise for the Princess.

He listened, then he said:

"No wonder you are rebellious! If I am not mistaken, Paulina, your account with the Maison Claré is astronomical. I know that *Monsieur* de Clermont-Tonnerre was complaining about it only the other day."

"My Chamberlain complains about everything I spend," the Princess said, pouting. "I am quite certain Napoleon has told him that I must economise, though why Heaven knows!"

She turned her face towards Vernita.

"And what, girl, are you asking for this négligée in which this gentleman tells me I look like an angel?"

Vernita named a sum which was exactly half what she knew the Maison Claré would charge.

"I am sure it is a bargain," the Princess said lightly. "What else can you make me—and quickly?"

"What does Your Imperial Highness need?"

"I need everything! New nightgowns—I am sick of all the ones I have! Chemises, handkerchiefs—anything that is new and lovely like this négligée I will buy from you as soon as it is completed."

"Thank you . . . thank you!" Vernita said almost breathlessly.

"Then start at once and do not keep me waiting," the Princess ordered imperiously.

"I will do that," Vernita said, "and please, *Madame la Princesse,* may I be paid at once? Not only do I need the money, but I will also have to buy new materials, laces, ribbons, and muslin."

The Princess gave an indifferent wave of her hand.

"See my Chamberlain or his Secretary. Do not worry me with such unimportant matters."

"Yes, *Madame,* of course, *Madame!*"

Vernita curtseyed again and moved towards the door.

This was wonderful! It was even better than she had expected! Now her mother could have the milk she needed, a chicken, and other nourishing food.

She opened the door, then as she stepped out into the Hall she suddenly felt overcome with excitement at what she had been promised.

Everything seemed to be going black, the floor rising up towards her.

She leaned against the wall, fighting against a faintness which made her feel dizzy and a coldness which seemed to invade her whole body.

Then she heard a deep voice behind her saying:

"Are you ill, *Mademoiselle?*"

It was impossible for her to see anything, but she knew that the gentleman who had been in the Salon with the Princess was speaking, the man whom she had called Axel.

"I . . . I am . . . all right," she tried to say, then felt his arm round her as he assisted her to a seat.

She put her hands up to her face, ashamed of her weakness, and she heard him giving an order to a servant before he said:

"Put your head down as low as you can onto your knees."

She obeyed him weakly, and his voice seemed to come from a very long distance away. . . .

It seemed only a few seconds later, although it might have been longer, when he said in an authoritative tone:

"Drink this."

She felt his arm supporting her as with difficulty she raised her head. Then there was the aroma of cognac and the fire of it passing down her throat.

She gasped and because it seemed to burn her the tears came into her eyes.

"No more . . . please . . . no more," she begged.

"Just one more sip," he said, and because it was too much effort to argue she did as he suggested.

The cognac swept away the darkness—she no longer felt faint and there was a new warmth inside her.

She raised her head to look at him.

"I ... am sorry," she managed to say.

He looked down at her for a moment before he asked:

"When did you last have anything to eat?"

"I ... I am ... all right now ... thank you."

"I asked you a question."

"I ... I was not ... hungry this morning."

"Then you ate last night," he said, "and I imagine if you did it was very little."

Her eyes dropped before his and the colour rose in her cheeks.

She was ashamed that she should be causing such a disturbance, but she supposed it sprang from her relief when the Princess bought the négligée from her and she knew there would be food for her mother and many other things that she needed so badly.

The gentleman beside her bent down and put his hand under her arm.

"Come with me," he said.

Because there was nothing else Vernita could do she obeyed him, and he led her across the Hall and into a Salon on the other side.

As he did so he spoke to a flunkey.

"Bring coffee and *croissants* as quickly as you can!"

"Very good, *Monsieur*," the footman replied.

Vernita was escorted to a sofa. She sat down and as she did so she said:

"I am ... sorry to be such a ... bother, and I am ... all right now ... I really am. I ... I think I should ... go home."

"Not until you have had something to eat," the gentleman answered.

He walked across the room to stand at the window.

"I have seen starvation too often not to recognise it," he said quietly. "Surely you have someone to look after you?"

"I have to ... look after my mother," Vernita answered. "She is ... ill and we are very ... poor."

The gentleman did not speak. A few minutes later the door opened and the footman came in with a tray on which was a silver coffee-pot and a covered dish of hot *croissants*.

"Will there be anything else, *Monsieur?*" the footman asked.

"Not for the moment," the gentleman replied, "but tell the Secretary of *Monsieur* de Clermont-Tonnerre that this young woman requires . . ."

He paused and looked at Vernita.

"How many *francs* did you say?" he asked.

She told him in a faint voice, feeling very embarrassed, and the gentleman repeated it to the flunkey.

The man disappeared and because there was no point in waiting she poured out some coffee, then took one of the *croissants* from the dish. She was in fact extremely hungry.

She had been hungry so often and for so long that now it had become a dull ache inside her and she had an almost perpetual headache that felt like a bar of iron across her forehead.

As soon as she began to eat, the pain began to lift, and having finished the *croissant* she drank the coffee and felt as if it brought life back into her body.

She did not realise that the gentleman was watching her, but now he said:

"Eat another one—you need it."

She looked at him, a little smile in her eyes.

"I . . . it seems . . . greedy."

"It would be stupid to waste them. If you leave them they will doubtless be thrown away."

She put out her hand with its long thin fingers.

"I . . . often think of the . . . waste there is in these big . . . houses, especially at . . . night when I am feeling . . . empty inside."

She did not know why it was easy to speak in such a way to the man who was with her.

Then even as she said the words she thought that for a seamstress it was out of character and would seem to him an impertinence.

'I have been so long without the company of people of my own class that I forgot I should be servile and respectful,' she thought. 'A seamstress should not speak to a friend of Her Imperial Highness in such a manner.'

But, strangely, he did not seem to mind.

"Hunger has a different effect on almost everybody," he said. "Some merely sink into a weakness in which they cannot think or even understand. Others have hallucinations. Some have strange dreams."

"It seems so ... mundane, somehow, to ... dream of food," Vernita replied. "We should be like the Saints ... fasting to fix our minds on higher things."

The gentleman laughed.

"You have forgotten the temptations of Saint Anthony which doubtless came from fasting, and I am quite sure the devils, demons, and bogies that a great number of the Saints saw all came because they were empty inside."

"I think that is ... rather disillusioning," Vernita answered. "I like to think that the Saints were invested with special powers not vouchsafed to us, and that their visions were real."

Again she thought this was a strange conversation, and because she was suddenly afraid he might be suspicious of her she drank her coffee and put down the cup.

"I am very grateful ... *Monsieur.*"

Even as she spoke the door opened and the flunkey appeared with a silver salver on which were the *francs* which the gentleman had asked for.

"The Secretary of *Monsieur le Chambellan* would like a receipt," he said.

"Yes ... of course," Vernita said, "and I should have given you the account."

She realised she had forgotten it because she was feeling so faint. Now she opened her bag and took out the bill which she had compiled on a piece of paper before she left home.

She looked round and seeing a writing-desk against one wall went to it and taking up the white

quill-pen which stood beside the ink-pot she signed
the receipt and put it on the silver salver.

Then she took the money with a little feeling of
delight and placed it in her bag.

The flunkey went from the room and she said a
little shyly to the gentleman, who had been watching her:

"I am very grateful, *Monsieur*, very grateful indeed!"

"You still look a little shaky," he said. "I will take
you home."

"No. No . . . of course not," she protested. "It is
quite . . unnecessary."

"I insist," he said. "I have a feeling that despite
the fact that you have had something to eat you
might collapse in the street."

"I promise you I shall be . . . all right."

"It is a waste of time to argue with me," he replied, and he was smiling.

Feeling that he overpowered her and it was impossible to argue, Vernita followed him as he walked
into the Hall and gave an order to one of the footmen.

There was a chaise drawn by two horses waiting
in the courtyard, and the footman beckoned a groom
who drove it to the front door.

"Will you get in?" the gentleman asked Vernita.

She looked at him wide-eyed, wanting to protest,
and yet knowing that anything she might say would
be swept aside imperiously.

Then as if he commanded her and she could not
disobey, she stepped into the chaise. He got into the
driving-seat beside her, taking up the reins, while
the groom perched up behind them.

They drove slowly round the courtyard and cut
through the entrance into the Rue du Faubourg Saint
Honoré.

"Where do you live?" he asked.

"A small street called the Rue des Arbres. It is
not far. It is off the Boulevard des Capucines. If you
put me down at the corner I can walk the rest of the
way."

"You can hardly expect me to behave in such a cavalier fashion."

"It is ... very kind of you ... and I am very grateful."

"What is your name?"

"V-Vernita ... Bernier."

There was a little pause before she said the second word and she was afraid he might have noticed it, but he answered:

"Mine is Storvik—Count Axel de Storvik, if you wish to be formal!"

"Then you are not French?"

"No, I am Swedish."

"I thought somehow you did not look French."

"You were right, but although you do not look particularly French I do not question your nationality."

"My ... father came from ... Normandy."

It was what Vernita thought she must say if she was ever questioned.

People who came from Normandy were fair-skinned and although her hair was not fair it did not have the darkness of that of most French girls.

The Count did not reply, he merely glanced at her for a moment. Then his eyes went back to his horses.

Because Vernita wished to change the subject from herself she asked:

"Do you like being in Paris?"

"It is very amusing," the Count answered, but he did not sound particularly amused.

"Have you always lived here?" he asked after they had driven a little farther.

"For some years," Vernita answered him truthfully. "We used to live in the country."

"I felt somehow that, looking as you do, you would prefer the country."

She glanced at him in surprise.

It was not the sort of remark, she thought, that the Count should make to a poor seamstress.

She could hardly believe that he was trying to

flirt with her, but one never knew. Her mother had warned her so often to be careful and not to get herself involved with strange men.

But the Count had been kind, so very kind, and Vernita could not think why he should bother himself with her.

She felt as if her heart was beating unaccountably fast and told herself it was due to the cognac and the coffee.

Now they were moving down the Boulevard des Capucines and she said:

"The Rue des Arbres is the last turning on the left before you get to the Avenue l'Opera."

The Count turned his horses with an expertise that she could not help admiring. Then they were in the narrow, rather squalid little Rue des Arbes and because she knew he was waiting for her to direct him Vernita said:

"It is the . . . next house on the left."

The Count pulled his horses to a standstill.

"Again, thank you very much indeed, *Monsieur*," Vernita said. "You have been so gracious and sympathetic and I shall never forget it!"

She put out her hand without thinking and the Count pulled off his riding-glove and took it in his.

"Take care of yourself, *Mademoiselle* Bernier," he said. "I feel it is something you have been neglecting to do . . ."

He would have finished the sentence, but at that moment Louise Danjou came tearing through the door of the house and across the pavement.

"*M'mselle,* we have been waiting for you!" she cried. "Hurry upstairs—your mother is ill—very ill— and Mama is with her!"

Vernita gave a little cry, sprang out of the chaise, and started to run as quickly as she could into the house.

Chapter Two

Princess Paulina was having her bath.

At ten o'clock in the morning a maid drew the curtains of her bed-room on the first floor and she awoke in her small bed draped with pink embroidered muslin.

In the adjoining room her Negro servant, Paul, prepared her bath.

Like all the Bonapartes, Paulina had a mania for bathing, and whenever possible she bathed in milk because she thought it improved her complexion and the texture of her skin.

Her bathroom was small with a low ceiling and the bath itself stood in an alcove.

Paulina would lie for a long time relaxing in the carefully heated water mixed with five gallons of milk.

She had however discovered that milk left a disagreeable odour; so Paul would go up a back-staircase to a small room above the bathroom and when he was ordered to do so would pour clear water down through a specially made opening onto Paulina below.

While she was in her bath the Princess sometimes permitted a few of her favourite admirers and lovers to be present; but this morning she was alone and after about five minutes she called out:

"Paul!"

The Negro, who was just outside the bathroom door, entered.

"Fetch *Monsieur le Comte!*" Paulina ordered, and the man hurried away to find Count Axel.

Only a few minutes passed before the Count entered the room.

He had been expecting the summons, knowing that nobody except himself had called at the Hôtel de Charost that morning and the Princess disliked being on her own.

She was, he was aware, interested in little but herself and the beauty of her body and she felt nothing but pride in revealing the latter to admiring eyes.

Now as the Count entered the bathroom Paul brought him a chair, and he sat looking to where in the alcove the Princess lay back in the opaque liquid.

She was looking extremely beautiful with her long dark hair swept out of sight in one of the little *boudoir*-caps she affected with bows of pink ribbon hiding her ears.

The Count knew that although her body was perfect in every other way the Princess had one defect.

There had been plenty of jealous women eager to tell him of an incident which had happened some years previously when he had himself not been present.

That winter Paulina had gained recognition as the most beautiful woman in Paris, and, always susceptible to flattery, she became increasingly conscious of her power especially where men were concerned.

But her throne was being disputed by a *Madame* de Contades, daughter of the *Marquis* de Bouille, who had helped Louis XVI to make his unsuccessful flight from Paris.

Madame de Contades also had a goddess-like head with luxuriant dark hair and flashing eyes.

She disliked Napoleon intensely, disparaged his military victories, and refused categorically to admit the exceptional beauty of his sister the *Citizeness Leclerc*, as Paulina was then known.

A Ball was being given by *Madame* Permon, who invited her own friends, the elite of the Faubourg St. Germain, and the Bonapartes.

It was to be one of the highlights of the Season and Paulina prepared for it almost as carefully as her brother prepared for a battle.

She went into long consultations with the best hairdresser and the most fashionable dressmaker in Paris to ensure that her entrance on the night of the Ball would be sensational.

She even asked *Madame* Permon's permission to change in her house before the Ball so that no-one would see her until she appeared advancing slowly across the Ball-Room to a seat which had been kept for her.

After hours of making decisions, cancellations, and redecisions, she finally chose a short-sleeved white Grecian tunic with a deep border of gold which was held up on her shoulders by cameos.

It displayed her lovely figure without much concealment and beneath her breasts she wore a golden girdle with a huge antique stone as a clasp.

On her arms glistened bracelets of gold and cameos, and her hair piled on top of her head was crowned with little bunches of golden grapes.

When she appeared, everyone in the Ball-Room gasped at her beauty and paid her fulsome compliments and tributes of admiration.

But *Madame* de Contades was seething with anger and jealousy.

When finally Paulina was reclining on a long sofa, in her favourite pose, *Madame* Permon moved across the room on the arm of her partner.

At first she complimented her rival on her appearance. Then she gave a start and said to her escort in a loud whisper which everyone could hear:

"What a pity that so lovely a creature should be so deformed! If I had such ugly ears I really think I would cut them off!"

Everyone's eyes turned towards Paulina's ears.

Apparently no-one had ever noticed them before, but in fact they were small, shapeless, and without any curl to them.

Paulina had retired, weeping, to *Madame* Permon's *boudoir,* and forever afterwards she kept her ears concealed by her hair, jewels, bows of ribbon, or a bandeau.

Now in her milk-bath, as she smiled at the Count it seemed that no man could perceive anything but her almost overwhelming beauty, yet there was that cynical look in his eyes and a twist to his lips which Vernita had noticed the previous day.

"I want your advice, Axel."

"What about?" the Count enquired.

"Those spiteful women who never leave me alone have thought of a new stick with which to beat me."

"Another?"

"Do they ever stop criticising and defaming me?" Paulina asked.

"What is it this time?"

He was well aware that the Princess was trying to act less outrageously than usual because she had been so thankful for being allowed to come back to Paris.

She had hated Italy and Napoleon had been forced to write to her continually, telling her she must have the good sense to conform to the manners and customs of the city of Rome and not show her distaste for the people.

He had always written sternly in his letters, and Paulina had screamed with fury and found it almost unbearable when she read:

> *Love your husband and his family. Be obliging and amiable, and do not count on me for help if at your age you let yourself be governed by bad advice. As for Paris, be assured you will find no support here; for I shall never receive you without your husband.*
>
> *If you fall out with Camillo it will be entirely your own fault and then France will be forbidden you. You will lose your happiness and my friendship.*

Finally, just before his Coronation, Napoleon had relented, giving Paulina permission to return to Paris.

But she had still been terrified that when it was over he might force her to return with her husband to Rome.

Prince Camillo Borghese had followed his wife to Paris for the Coronation, but now he spoke of returning home.

Paulina was in abject despair that she might be obliged to go with him.

She besought Napoleon on her knees to save her, and because he could not remain angry with his favourite sister for long, he found a solution to her problem.

He realised that if Prince Camillo was given French nationality it would absolve Paulina from having to live in Italy, and accordingly Napoleon had given him a commission as a Colonel in the mounted Grenadier Guards which were encamped at Boulogne.

In return Napoleon insisted on Paulina behaving in a manner which was in keeping with her new position as an Imperial Highness.

He was well aware of how unrestrained and indeed in many ways how uncivilised she was, but he was determined that she should be an asset to the new *Régime* he was forming, which he hoped would make him respected by the other Crowned Heads of Europe.

He told her that she should have a household of her own and her own Court, but she had no say in the appointments, which were all made by Napoleon himself or by the Grand Marshal of his household.

Everything had been done with an eye to impressing the aristocratic families of the Faubourg St. Germain.

Paulina's Chamberlain, *Monsieur* de Clermont-Tonnerre, was the impoverished head of an illustrious and aristocratic family.

His social qualifications were unequalled, and he was, the Count had found, a pleasant, good-humoured man, much liked by the majority of the household.

The Princess's Chief Equerry, Louis de Mont-breton, was already extremely enamoured of his mistress and as he was lively and versatile he was undoubtedly an asset to her entourage.

Paulina had also been given two attractive and distinguished Ladies-in-Waiting—besides a *Dame d'Honneur* who the Princess decided immediately on her arrival was a bore.

However, she liked *Mademoiselle* Mills, her *lectrice* or reader, who was not only intelligent but had written a popular historical novel.

Other posts in the Princess's official establishment included a Physician, an Armourer, two Chaplains, a Secretary, a Chief Steward, and a Pharmacist. They filled the Hôtel de Charost.

While this made an excellent front for the world, there was always the unpredictability of the Princess herself and her endless capacity for getting into trouble, which kept the household on tenterhooks and Napoleon worried.

"What have you done now?" the Count enquired.

"It is not what I have done," the Princess snapped, "but what they are saying about me."

"What are they saying?"

"Some of those stuck-up women who dare to criticise me—and I am sure that the odious *Madame* de Contades is at the bottom of it—say that it is indecent for Paul to carry me to and from my bath."

The Count smiled.

He had already heard some very ribald remarks about the Princess's behaviour in allowing a Negro to be brought into such intimate contact with her body.

It was not so much indolence, he knew, but the pleasure that Paulina enjoyed from the contrast between her pearl-like skin and that of her black servant.

"A Negro is not like other men," the Princess was saying positively. "Or do you think they are shocked because he is young and unmarried? Well, I can soon arrange that!"

The Count did not speak and she said:

"He can marry one of the kitchen-maids. I will send for one and tell them they are to marry each other."

"The woman may object," the Count remarked.

"She will do as she is told or I will dismiss her!" Paulina retorted.

"I thought you were going to ask my advice."

"I was, but you have made up my mind for me without my having to listen to you," the Princess remarked irrepressibly.

She smiled and added:

"Now let us talk of something else. Servants are always a boring subject, and you have not yet told me I am looking beautiful."

"That goes without saying," the Count replied. "You look lovely, as you are well aware."

He spoke nothing but the truth and Paulina was smiling as she said:

"Go on!"

"What do you want to hear?" he enquired. "That your skin is like a pearl set in the Milky Way?"

Paulina laughed.

"That is quite perceptive of you, Axel. I much prefer your compliments to those of the French gallants which sound as glib as if they have uttered them a hundred times already, which of course they have!"

The Count smiled.

"I am sure you would be disappointed if they talked of someone else."

"But of course!" Paulina agreed. "Who could be more interesting than I?"

"I was thinking that you should have a négligée which would make you look even more entrancing than you do at the moment," Count Axel said slowly.

Paulina turned her face towards him.

She was always attentive when someone spoke of clothes.

"Perhaps one of white," the Count suggested, "touched with silver and lined with the faintest pink to reflect your skin."

Paulina sat up in the bath, revealing her perfectly curved, rose-tipped breasts.

"Axel, you are a genius!" she cried. "It would be fascinating and at the same time extremely alluring! Why did I not think of it?"

"You cannot see yourself as I see you," the Count replied.

"We will order one when we go downstairs," Paulina said. "White and silver, lined with pink—and of course silver ribbons in my hair."

She called out:

"The shower, Paul!" and the Count heard the Negro's footsteps padding away towards the backstairs.

"Who will you get to make this garment?" the Count asked as the Princess stood up in the bath so that she was underneath the hole in the ceiling through which the water would descend.

"Who else but the woman who made my other négligée?" she replied. "Send a servant for her straight away. I want her. I want her here as quickly as possible!"

"That may be difficult," the Count replied doubtfully.

"Difficult?" Paulina enquired. "But why?"

As she spoke to him she was putting a cap over her head which would prevent the shower from wetting her hair.

"The seamstress who brought your négligée yesterday," the Count answered, "collapsed when she left the room—I think through lack of food. Because I felt sorry for her I sent her home in my chaise."

"Well, she will have recovered by now," Paulina remarked indifferently.

"My groom tells me that when she arrived back at the house where she lives she learnt that her mother was dead," the Count continued. "I thought that perhaps, in the circumstances, she would give

up her work and move to the country to live with relations."

Paulina gave a little scream of fury.

"*Pardi!*" she exclaimed. "That is something that
certainly must not happen. I need her! I want her!
There is no-one else who sews as well as she does.
Get her here immediately and I will persuade her to
stay in Paris and work for me."

"Supposing she refuses?" the Count asked.

"Then I will have her kidnapped, imprisoned—
held by some means, whatever it may be."

Paulina stamped her foot in the water and
added:

"Stop arguing with me, Axel, and order a servant
to fetch her. I will tell her what she is to do."

The Count rose slowly from his chair.

He was about to say something else but at that
moment the water poured by Paul splashed down onto Paulina and it was obvious that she would be unable to hear what he was saying.

There was a faint smile on his lips as he went
down the stairs to order his chaise.

*   *   *

When Vernita had left Count Axel the day before and run across the pavement and up the stairs
of the tall house with its grey shutters, he had turned
to Louise, who was standing there staring at the
chaise and the horses with admiring eyes.

"What has occurred?" he enquired.

"*Madame* Bernier is dead," the girl answered.
"My mother went upstairs to take her a cup of coffee
and found that she had died while *M'mselle* was out."

"That is tragic!" the Count exclaimed. "I wonder, is there anything I can do to help?"

He gave the reins to the groom and walked up
to the door of the house.

"On which floor does *Mademoiselle* reside?" he
enquired of Louise, who had followed him.

"Right at the top, *Monsieur.* It is a climb of four
flights!"

"I dare say I can manage it," the Count replied.

He started up the narrow stairway, noting that when he reached the third floor the carpet ceased and there were only wooden boards on which to walk.

The door of the attic room which was occupied by Vernita and her mother was open, and standing in the entrance he could see Vernita kneeling beside the bed.

By the window *Madame* Danjou was crying into her handkerchief.

The Count stood for a moment looking at the dead woman with her white hair framing her thin face with its sensitive features. Her eyes were closed but he thought that she looked unexpectedly happy.

Vernita was crying helplessly, like a child, and not liking to disturb her he beckoned to *Madame* Danjou, who followed him from the room onto the landing, shutting the door behind her.

"Is there anything I can do?" the Count asked in a low voice.

"It is so sad, *Monsieur*. The poor lady. She seemed to waste away," *Madame* Danjou said, the tears running down her fat cheeks.

"They are very poor?" the Count asked, thinking of the empty, cheerless attic with nothing to soften its austerity.

"*Très pauvres, Monsieur,*" *Madame* Danjou replied. "Often they would not have had enough to eat if I had not helped them."

"I am sure you were very kind," the Count answered. "And now there will be the expense of a funeral."

Madame Danjou shrugged her shoulders expressively.

The Count drew some gold coins from his pocket.

"Pay for what is necessary," he said, "and I will return tomorrow and see if I can be of further help to *Mademoiselle*. Do not let her leave without seeing me."

"She will not do that, *Monsieur*," *Madame* Danjou answered. "There is nowhere for her to go."

"She has no friends or relatives?"

"None that I ever heard of or saw," *Madame* replied.

"I will return tomorrow," the Count repeated, and went down the stairs, leaving *Madame* Danjou staring in surprise at the gold coins in her hand.

While returning to the Hôtel de Charost he had continuously been trying to think of a way in which he could help Vernita.

Now he knew he had something concrete to suggest to her.

He made no attempt to send a servant as the Princess had suggested, but drove himself towards the Rue des Arbres.

He knew Paulina would not miss him, for after her bath she always sat before a mirror in her bed-room, wearing only a chemise, while a maid arranged her dark hair.

There would be a long discussion as to what style she should choose, and often when it was completed Paulina would change her mind and her hair would have to be done all over again.

After that, it always took time for her to apply her make-up.

She used almond paste, cucumber salve, and *lait de rose*, besides a special Oriental preparation which darkened her lashes and eye-brows.

After this an attar of roses was sprayed by her maid all over her white body before she chose the delectable *déshabillé* in which she would receive her morning visitors.

The Count was well aware that he could get to the Rue des Arbres and back again long before Paulina came downstairs to the *Boudoir Violet*, where the tradesmen would be waiting with their wares.

Then she would move into her favourite Salon, next to the State *Boudoir*.

In the bed-room, the elaborately carved bed

stood on a dais. The gilt crown was surmounted by
an eagle and garnished with twenty-six ostrich-feathers.

The exterior of the canopy of the bed was up-
holstered in blue, the interior in white satin woven
with gold rosettes.

On the walls of the room, blue voile embroidered
with gold was draped and encircled by motifs of gilt
myrtle leaves—the emblem of Venus.

Paulina seldom slept all night in this seductive
room, but used it for the romantic interludes which
she craved with all her passionate, emotional nature.

It was a tragedy, the Count thought, that the
Prince Camillo, who loved and admired his wife,
should be, unlike most Italians, an indifferent lover.

He was pleasant enough, peaceable and good-
humoured, but his passions were expended on horses
and carriages.

Paulina made no secret to her friends that she
found him intolerably dull.

Laure Junot, wife of General Andoche Junot, who
had been made Governor of Paris when he was
twenty-nine, could not resist telling how immediately
after Paulina and Camillo were married she had been
invited to travel with them from St. Cloud to Paris.

She had suggested that as they were on honeymoon she might be *de trop.*

"A honeymoon with that imbecile?" Paulina had
exclaimed. "What on earth are you thinking of?"

The Count drove his horses in and out of the
quite considerable traffic in the Boulevard des Capucines.

Spring was always particularly attractive in Paris
and the flower-sellers' baskets were vivid with the
colours of carnations from the South, great bunches
of Parma violets, narcissuses, daffodils, and lilies,
which would be in great demand at Easter.

In contrast to the bustle, colour, and excitement
of the Boulevards, the Rue des Arbres looked even
more squalid and dismal than it had the day before.

The tall houses on either side of the narrow street kept out the sunshine and the Count looked with distaste at the dirty roadway and the unswept pavement.

He brought his horses to a standstill outside the house where Vernita was lodging, and finding the front door open he entered the narrow Hall.

There was the smell of cooking floating up from the basement; and as there seemed to be no sign of anyone about, the Count began to climb the long flights of stairs as he had done the previous day.

He had reached the third-floor landing when he saw Vernita coming down the stairs towards him, and stopped to wait until she reached where he was standing.

"Good morning, *Mademoiselle*," he said, sweeping his high-crowned hat from his dark head.

She dropped him a curtsey, then looked up at him with wide, questioning eyes.

She was even paler than she had been the day before, and her eyes, almost dark purple, seemed to the Count to be pools of despair.

She was not wearing black, as he had seen her yesterday, but a mauve gown which reminded him of the violets that were on sale on the Boulevards.

It was a simple gown, and yet, being experienced in the ways of women, he knew that while it was not quite new, it was of good material and must once have been expensive.

"*Madame* Danjou said that you ... might call to see . . . me," Vernita said in a voice that trembled.

"May I tell you how sorry I am about your mother," the Count said.

He saw the tears come into her eyes and she looked away from him.

"Mama died because we could not earn enough money to buy the food she needed," Vernita replied.

There was in her soft voice a bitter note which the Count had not heard before.

"I am very sorry," he said quietly.

"She suffered so much during the cold winter months, but in a way I think she is happy to be with Papa."

She spoke simply, almost as if she spoke to herself, and the Count replied gently:

"I thought when I saw your mother yesterday that she looked happy, as if she had found what she was seeking."

Vernita looked at him in astonishment and he explained:

"I followed you up the stairs. The young girl who called you into the house told me that your mother was dead."

"*Madame* Danjou told me how kind you were in giving her the money for the funeral. Mama was . . . buried this morning. They did not wish to have a . . . dead body for long in the house."

"I can understand that," the Count said. "But what do you intend now to do with yourself?"

There was a little pause and he felt that metaphorically she shrugged her shoulders.

"I can go on working," she said after a moment.

"From here?"

"I think *Madame* Danjou will allow me to keep the room."

"You will find it very lonely without your mother."

"I know," she answered, "but what else can I do?"

"That is something I am going to suggest to you."

She looked up at him again and he thought, although he was not sure, that she stiffened. Realising that she might misunderstand his words, he said quickly:

"I believe it would be possible to find you a position at the Hôtel de Charost."

Now her expression was one of astonishment, and he continued:

"The Princess appreciates your work. She has an order already waiting for you, and I am sure I could

arrange, if you would accept it, for you to live in the
house as officially her personal seamstress."

Vernita clasped her fingers together and stood
looking down the stairs as if she thought it could
somehow help her to understand and to appraise
the suggestion which had been made to her.

The Count, watching her, knew that she had
never contemplated such a thing, and she was be-
wildered and nervous at the idea of living in the
Hôtel de Charost.

He waited without speaking, looking very large
and out of place on the small landing in his fashionable champagne-coloured pantaloons and close-
fitting cut-away coat.

His white muslin cravat was intricately tied and
the points of his collar rose against the squareness of
his chin.

As if Vernita was suddenly aware of the contrast
he made to the squalid surroundings, she said in a
hesitating voice:

"It is . . . very kind of you . . . but I think perhaps
it would be . . . better for me to stay . . . here."

"You really think that is the right decision?" the
Count asked. "It will be cold and lonely and there
will be no-one to talk to except the woman and her
daughter whom I saw yesterday."

He felt that Vernita, although she concealed it,
gave a little shiver.

She had already thought how hard it would be to
live in this gloomy place without her mother.

She was also well aware that Louise would pes-
ter her, as she had done before, to go out with her
onto the streets at night and find young men with
whom they could amuse themselves.

Everything that was fastidious and well-bred in
Vernita shrank from contemplating anything which
would have horrified her mother, and also she knew
that it would be difficult to reiterate her refusals to
Louise over and over again.

"You would be wise to let me decide this for
you," the Count said in his deep voice.

"Why should you . . . want to do so?" Vernita asked. "Why should you . . . trouble yourself with me?"

She tried to sound proud and independent, but instead she sounded only helpless and nervous, as a child afraid of taking a step in the dark.

"I was sorry for you yesterday," the Count replied, "and realised you had been exploited by the shop that employed you. What I find most unpleasant about the French is that they are very avaricious."

"But . . . they can also be . . . kind," Vernita replied, thinking of *Madame* Danjou.

"Perhaps you will find them too kind if you live here alone," the Count said.

She glanced at him swiftly, then away again, and he knew that he had struck her on a vulnerable spot.

She was thinking of how apprehensive her mother had always been when she walked on the streets alone.

She was remembering little things she had experienced which she had never repeated to her mother—incidents of men speaking to her when she was shopping, and times when she felt terrified because there was no-one to protect her.

At least in a large house like the Hôtel de Charost, she thought, there would be other women-servants with whom she could associate and who would doubtless treat her as one of themselves.

Anything, she suddenly thought passionately, would be better than to live alone in the attic where she had once had the companionship of her mother, alone in the day, alone at night, and alone when she walked through the streets.

"Has the Princess said that she wants me?" she asked the Count.

"Not yet," he replied, "but she has sent me to find you as she wishes to order another négligée to be made for her immediately."

"Am I to come with you now?"

"At this moment! You will discover that when

Her Imperial Highness wants something, she wants it the second she has spoken; or if possible before she has even thought of it!"

His joke brought a faint smile to Vernita's lips. Then she said:

"If you will be kind enough to wait for me downstairs, I will fetch my bonnet."

"Then hurry," the Count said.

He walked down the stairs, climbed into his chaise, and took the reins from his groom.

It was only a few minutes later that Vernita crossed the pavement to seat herself beside him.

He realised that she was wearing a very different headgear from what she had worn the day before.

Instead of the plain black straw hat that was worn by the type of young women who earned their own living, she was wearing a bonnet which he was certain had cost a lot of money.

It was very plain, trimmed only with pale mauve ribbons to match Vernita's gown, but there was something about it which altered her appearance and made her look, the Count thought, exactly like the lady he was quite certain she was.

As if she knew what he was thinking, Vernita said:

"I ... I had no time to ... change."

She paused, and then as if she felt she must be honest she added:

"Yesterday I ... borrowed the clothes I was wearing from *Madame* Danjou's daughter. Today I did not like to ask for them again. This is all I have."

She did not add that the gown was in fact her mother's, who had liked mauve as a colour, and it was the nearest thing to mourning which Vernita could find amongst what remained of their wardrobe.

Everything that was valuable, like their furs, had been sold, but there had been no point in disposing of their gowns when they would have to be replaced.

Deep in the bottom of the two trunks standing in the attic were their evening-dresses for which there would be no sale but which were all made in expensive materials.

Vernita had thought that perhaps one day she would make them into something useful, but in the meantime there were a number of pretty, elegant day-gowns which they had brought to Paris in the spring two years ago.

She was well aware that she looked different from how a seamstress should look, but she had nothing else to wear.

If the Princess refused to employ her on account of her clothes, then there would be nothing she could do but go back to live alone in the attic.

"Suppose you tell me about yourself?" the Count suggested unexpectedly.

She had an unaccountable impulse to do as he asked and explain the horrible fate that had overtaken her and her family when Napoleon had thrown all the British tourists into prison.

Yet, how could she tell him the truth without finding herself in prison?

Although the Count might be Swedish, he was obviously friendly with the avowed enemies of the English and there would be no question of where his loyalty lay.

"I told you ... yesterday," Vernita said. "My father came from ... Normandy, but we have lived in Paris for the last two or three years."

"What did your father do?"

Vernita's imagination was struggling to make any story she told sound truthful and plausible.

"He had an interest in various different things," she answered vaguely, "but I am afraid Papa was not a good businessman and had merely been brought up to ... enjoy himself."

This was true, she thought.

"And when he died he left you and your mother with very little money?"

Vernita sighed.

"I think perhaps Papa was ... unlucky at cards."

This she knew was a very reasonable excuse, for

she had learnt when they first came to Paris how everyone gambled.

There were not only cards and games of chance for the rich but lotteries for the poor, and the hope of making a fortune by a twist of the cards or a number on a piece of paper created an almost fanatical belief in fate.

"So he was a gambler!" the Count said quietly.

"I am . . . afraid so."

Her father had told her of the gambling which took place in the Palais Royal, where fortunes were squandered on the green-baize tables every night.

She knew too that at the Balls and parties they had attended there were always gentlemen who withdrew from the glittering throng, finding the glint of a golden louis more inviting than the glint in some beautiful woman's eyes.

"So he left you and your mother very little," the Count said. "Have you no relations or friends with whom you could live now?"

"Living in Paris, we lost . . . touch with those whom we . . . knew in the . . . country," Vernita answered.

It sounded quite plausible, she thought, and only hoped they would soon reach the Hôtel de Charost so that the Count would stop asking her questions.

"I can see," he said almost as if he were speaking to himself, "that being alone at your age and being so attractive will present problems wherever you go."

"I hope not," she said quickly.

"You know it is true," he insisted, "and I will try to help you, but you know that ultimately you will have to look after yourself."

"Yes, of course. I am aware of that."

"Then be careful," he said. "Be careful what you do and what you say, and try not to look so lovely."

She turned her face to stare at him wide-eyed.

It seemed such an extraordinary thing for him to say.

"I am serious," the Count said. "You are in Paris and it is the one Capital in Europe where a

pretty woman is appreciated. But that also con-
stitutes dangers of its own."

Now Vernita understood and knew he was warning her, but against whom?

They turned into the Rue du Faubourg Saint
Honoré and there was no time for the Count to question her further. But she knew that he had spoken
seriously, almost solemnly, and she told herself as
they drove round the courtyard to the front door of
the Hôtel de Charost that she must pay attention to
what he said.

She stepped out and realised that the flunkey
did not recognise her in the clothes she was wearing
today and assisted her with the obsequious attention
he would have accorded to one of the Princess's
guests.

The Count handed his hat and gloves to another
flunkey and walked across the Hall to open the door
into the *boudoir* where Vernita had seen the Princess
Paulina the previous day.

There were three people in the room who
were all obviously shop-keepers, and the Count
closed the door without suggesting that Vernita should
join them.

Instead he indicated a small sofa at the far end
of the Hall near the stairs.

"Wait there!" he said, and climbed the stairs,
leaving her alone.

She sat primly on the edge of the sofa, her hands
clasped in her lap.

The four footmen, with their powdered wigs, on
duty in the Hall glanced at her surreptitiously but
made no attempt to speak, and she knew that they
were puzzled as to why she was there.

They were too well-trained to appear inquisitive
and they merely stood in silence, their gold-braided
green livery over white breeches making them appear very resplendent.

The Count found the Princess Paulina as he had
expected in her bed-room.

She was nearly ready and wearing the négligée that Vernita had brought her the day before.

With its pale rose-coloured muslin bows and ecru-coloured lace she looked extremely attractive, and as if pleased with her reflection she turned to the Count with a smile that was already on her lips.

"Where have you been, Axel?" she asked. "I wanted you to talk to me while I was dressing."

"I was carrying out your orders," he replied in a deliberately grudging tone.

She gave a little exclamation.

"Of course! I sent you to find the woman who would make my white and silver négligée."

"It is just like you to send me on an unpleasant errand and then forget what I am doing."

"You found her?"

"Of course! Do I ever fail you?"

"And she is here?"

"Downstairs, waiting for you."

"Oh, good! I have thought of several other things I want."

"The woman cannot be expected to make more than one garment at a time," the Count remarked.

"Then she will have to try!" the Princess replied petulantly. "You complained about the nightgown I was wearing last night, so I have thrown it away. You were right, it was unbecoming."

Because the Count was looking sullen, the Princess crossed the room to put her hands on his shoulders and gaze up into his eyes.

She was so small that she reached only to his shoulders.

"Do not be cross, Axel," she begged. "I am grateful to you for fetching the woman I wanted, and think how much it will delight you when you see me looking beautiful in the things she will make for me."

"If she does!" the Count replied.

The Princess stiffened.

"What do you mean? She can hardly refuse my orders."

"I told you that her mother is dead. I discovered that she intends to leave Paris because she has nowhere to stay. It is not easy to find cheap accommodation in the city at the moment."

The Princess gave a little laugh.

"Is that all? Well, the solution is easy. She can stay here!"

The Count looked surprised.

"I never thought of that."

"You are so impractical, *mon cher!*" the Princess replied. "Now that you have brought the woman here, leave everything to me. You know if I want something I have to have it."

She sounded like a spoilt child and the Count laughed, then taking her chin in his fingers he turned her face up to his.

"One day you will ask for the moon," he said, "and be quite surprised when it does not fall into your arms!"

"But it will," the Princess answered.

The Count kissed her classical little nose.

"I know now why the Bonapartes have conquered a quarter of the world," he said.

"Only a quarter?" the Princess queried. "What can Napoleon be thinking about? He told me he would conquer the whole!"

"There is still England."

"Who wants that tiresome little island?" the Princess asked petulantly, turning away from him.

"Your brother, for one," the Count replied.

"Then he will get it! Napoleon always gets what he wants," Paulina said, "and do not dare suggest otherwise!"

"As if I would be so impolite," the Count said with a smile.

"I think Napoleon is coming to see me tomorrow."

"Then I hope I shall be allowed to meet him."

Paulina laughed.

"You are still trying to interest him in that ridiculous gun of yours?"

"Why not? It could prove itself to be a very formidable weapon."

"If it works!" the Princess said scornfully. "I told Napoleon you wanted to show him the design and he said he has been given stacks of designs to inspect! But when the guns were made they fell to bits at the first salvo or proved too heavy to pull over the ground if it was muddy."

"There is nothing like that about my gun," the Count replied almost aggressively. "General Junot, to whom I showed it before he left for Portugal, was impressed with it and so was Marshal Ney!"

The Princess laughed again and, standing on tiptoe, put her arms round his neck and pulled his head down to hers.

"I adore you, Axel!" she said. "You excite me as no other man has been able to do before. After being married to that boring Camillo, who is little more than a eunuch, you thrill me!"

"Which of course is very gratifying," the Count said with a touch of sarcasm in his voice.

"But we must be careful, very careful," Paulina warned. "If Napoleon thinks we are being talked about, he will send you away. You know he does not approve of my having a lover."

"Then we must certainly be very careful," the Count said.

"That is not the right answer!" the Princess said sharply. "If you loved me you would stand up to Napoleon and defy him! After all, he is only my brother."

"And the Emperor!"

She made a grimace, but the Count knew she was frightened that Napoleon might bring her husband back to Paris to prevent a scandal.

"I want you to love me so much that nothing else is of importance," she insisted. "Napoleon said once that there is a magnetic fluid between two people who love each other. He was right."

"Of course," the Count agreed.

The Princess kissed him, her lips pressing against his, then she took her arms from round his neck.

"Let us go and order my négligée," she said, "and afterwards, when I have finished my morning's business, we can be alone."

"Why not?" the Count replied.

But the Princess had not waited to hear his reply. She was hurrying from the room towards the staircase which would lead her down to the *Boudoir Violet*, where she knew the dressmakers were waiting for her.

However much a lover excited her, however irresistible she found the man on whom she had set her fancy, there was one thing which took precedence over everything else, and that was the adornment of her exquisite body.

Chapter Three

Driving back with the Count, Vernita could not make up her mind if she was glad or frightened at what had been arranged.

The Princess had swept down the stairs, her diaphanous négligée doing little to conceal her beautiful body, and as she reached the Hall, the Count, walking behind her, had said in a quiet voice:

"*Mademoiselle* Bernier is here waiting for you."

"So I see," the Princess replied, and walking towards Vernita, who rose and curtseyed, she said sharply:

"It is all arranged, you will stay here. There is a great deal for you to do and I need you to start work immediately."

Vernita looked at her apprehensively, then said in a low voice.

"I have to pack, Your Imperial Highness. Could I . . . please come tomorrow?"

She did not know why she prevaricated, she just felt as if she were being swept along on a tide which was overwhelming her and she was finding it difficult to catch her breath.

"I suppose so," the Princess said grudgingly, "but I need my négligée immediately!"

She looked at the Count.

"Explain to this woman what you had in mind, Axel, and tomorrow she must bring me the materials so that we can ascertain that they are exactly what you want."

Her voice softened on the last two words and she looked at the Count in a manner which made Vernita lower her own eyes in embarrassment.

"You may leave everything to me," the Count said with a faint smile. "I thought I was an expert on guns, but now I have a second profession—négligée-designer!"

The Princess laughed.

"Very well, arrange it your own way, but if I am disappointed you will have to pay for it."

"It will be a privilege," the Count replied.

She laughed again and swept into the *Boudoir Violet,* where she knew the dressmakers were waiting for her.

"Come and help me choose a new gown for the Ball next week, Axel," she called over her shoulder as she reached the door.

"I will choose your dress as soon as I have finished choosing your undress," he replied, and she gave him one of her alluring smiles before she disappeared and the door shut behind her.

The Count looked at Vernita.

"I suppose," he said, as she did not speak, "that you will want some money to buy the materials which the Princess will require."

"Yes, please," she replied, "and what sort of négligée does Her Imperial Highness wish me to make?"

"Come with me and I will explain," the Count said.

He led the way to the small Salon where they had talked the day before.

As a flunkey closed the door behind them the Count said:

"I told the Princess that your mother is dead and that you were thinking of leaving Paris. It was therefore her suggestion that you should stay here."

"I am grateful... very grateful," Vernita replied, "but you will understand that it is all rather ... alarming."

She looked round at the elaborate furnishings of the room and thought what a startling contrast they were to the attic in which she had lived for the last two years.

"I know it will be difficult at first," the Count said, "and you will be expected to live with the servants, but it is better than starving in that appalling garret!"

"Yes, of course," Vernita agreed.

"Now tell me what money you require to purchase the materials for a négligée of white trimmed with touches of silver and lined with pink that is almost flesh-coloured."

"That sounds very attractive."

"It will be when you make it."

"I am afraid the materials will be expensive."

"That is of no consequence. I am going to see the Princess's Chamberlain or his Secretary and arrange that you can order the materials you want from any well-known shop."

He moved towards the door as he spoke, adding:

"Stay here until I return!"

When he had gone, Vernita sat down on an armchair.

She felt as if her head were in a whirl. She could hardly believe that this was all happening to her, and she knew that while in fact it offered a solution to her problems, it was at the same time a step into the unknown.

She would have been feeling even more apprehensive if she had realised that the reason why the Count had not taken her with him to meet *Monsieur* de Clermont-Tonnerre was that the Chamberlain had an eye for a pretty woman.

Vernita was looking so attractive that the Count had been half-afraid the Princess would refuse to employ her.

Fortunately, Paulina was concentrating entirely upon herself and he was certain that if she was asked she would have been quite unable to describe Vernita in any detail.

She was in fact unaware that she was looking any different from the previous day.

Then her black gown and plain straw hat had made her look unexpectedly attractive for a seamstress, but today the Count knew that, dressed as a Lady of Quality, he would have been proud to be seen with her in any of the fashionable parts of Paris.

When he came back from having made all the necessary arrangements not with the Chamberlain but with his Secretary, who kept the accounts appertaining to the household, he was wondering how he could tell her that she must change her appearance.

Then he told himself with one of his cynical smiles that it was not her clothes that should be altered but her face.

Vernita rose as he entered the Salon. Her eyes had an anxious expression in them and the Count was sure she had been worrying since he had left her.

"Everything is arranged," he said in a quiet voice.

He handed her three cards which bore the Princess's crest signed by the Chamberlain.

"These will enable you to order the materials you need from any well-known shop and the goods will be delivered here," he said.

"Thank you," Vernita replied.

"I have also arranged your salary," the Count continued. "You will receive eight hundred *francs* a year, payable monthly, and of course your board and lodging."

"That is too much!" Vernita gasped.

The Count smiled.

"I doubt if you will find that it goes very far in Paris," he replied, thinking of the wild extravagances of the Princess, who paid more than that for a new bonnet.

Then he remembered that, living as she had, Vernita would know exactly how far a *franc* would go, and he said:

"This is a Royal Household and the Emperor would not wish any member of it, high or low, to be paid inadequately."

"You know I am grateful," Vernita said.

"I will take you home," the Count suggested.

He opened the door to let Vernita precede him, and only as she reached the doorstep did she realise that in her position she should have followed him.

When they were driving down the Rue du Faubourg Saint Honoré she said in a low voice:

"I hope I shall not . . . fail and . . . disappoint you."

"It is the Princess you have to please—not me," the Count answered, "and I doubt if I shall be staying long in Paris."

His words made Vernita turn to look at him quickly, and she asked:

"You are going away?"

She did not know why, but she felt upset and apprehensive at the idea.

"I may have to return home at any moment," the Count answered. "That is why I would like to give you some good advice before I leave."

"I will listen to . . . anything you wish to . . . say."

"It is hard for us to talk here," the Count said, driving his horses down the Boulevard. "What I am going to suggest is that when you have finished your packing you have dinner with me tonight."

Vernita's expression turned to one of surprise.

This was somehow the last thing she expected him to say to her.

"D-dinner?" she said, faltering.

"It would be so much easier if we could talk together in some quiet Restaurant," the Count said.

"But . . . but . . . the Princess?"

Vernita was sure that the Princess would think it extremely reprehensible and positively insulting that the man she quite obviously fancied should take out one of her servants.

"The Princess will not know where we are," the Count answered. "She is in fact dining at a party to which I have not been invited."

Vernita was silent for a moment, then said:

"It would not be . . . wrong?"

She was not quite certain what she meant, except that it was utterly revolutionary for her to be asked out to dinner.

She had never dined alone with a man, and she had the feeling that her mother would have disapproved of her accepting such an invitation.

The Count appeared to consider her question, then he said:

"It would certainly not be wrong—unconventional, perhaps—but I am afraid I cannot think of a suitable Chaperon, and do we really need one?"

"No . . . I suppose . . . not," Vernita replied.

She was conscious that her heart was beating quickly and that though she was trying to consider the invitation sensibly there was a flicker of excitement rising within her which she could not suppress.

"Very well, then," the Count said. "I will call for you at seven o'clock."

They were travelling down the Rue des Arbres as he spoke, and Vernita said quickly:

"Please . . . what shall I wear?"

It was a feminine question which made him smile.

"We will go somewhere very quiet," he replied. "If you have a simple evening-gown, put it on; if not, what you are wearing at the moment is very charming."

"But unsuitable for my position," Vernita said. "I realised you were thinking that when we were at the Hôtel de Charost."

"I also thought," he replied, "that it would make very little difference what you wore, as it would be impossible for you to change the shape of your face and the size of your eyes."

She felt herself quiver at the note in his voice.

Then the horses came to a standstill and the groom jumped down from behind the chaise to help Vernita to alight.

"Seven o'clock," the Count said quietly, raising his hat.

Vernita did not look back as she walked across

the dirty pavement and into the dark, gloomy house.

Only as she reached the attic bed-room where she had lived for so long did she run to the trunks that stood against the wall.

She started to pull out the garments that lay at the bottom of them, frantically trying to discover something in which the Count would think she looked attractive.

* * *

The Count was punctual and Vernita was waiting downstairs for his horses to turn into the street.

The small Hall suddenly seemed so unpleasant that she wondered how she and her mother had been able to tolerate it for so long.

The paper was peeling from the walls and although there was a carpet on the stairs it was worn and sadly in need of being beaten.

As the Count had noticed, a smell of cooking was wafting up from the basement and there were various old coats and hats hung on a hat-stand by tenants who were too lazy to carry them up to their own apartments.

As the horses came to a standstill outside, Vernita saw that they were drawing not the chaise in which she had ridden with the Count in the morning, but in a closed carriage with both a coachman and a footman on the box.

The latter sprang down to open the door and the Count got out, so resplendent in his evening-clothes that Vernita drew in her breath.

It was a long time since she had last seen a gentleman looking so smart, and it made her think of the parties her father and mother attended when they had first reached Paris two years ago.

Nothing could have been more glamorous or more colourful, she had thought, than the levees and the Drawing-Rooms, and she had never forgotten an Assembly to which her father had taken her in the Tuileries.

The hundreds of footmen in their green and gold livery, the gorgeously begilt Palace Officials who paraded the Ante-Chambers, the pages with their gold chains and medallions, and the uniforms of the Aides-de-Camp had dazzled her.

The gentlemen who partnered her at the Balls had either worn uniforms with gold epaulettes or had seemed equally resplendent in their knee-breeches and long-tailed coats with white cravats in which glittered jewelled tie-pins that complemented their glittering fobs.

Now as the Count advanced across the pavement towards her, Vernita wished she had chosen a more elaborate gown than the one she was wearing.

Because she should really have been in mourning for her mother, she had refused to entertain the idea of putting on any gown that was blue or pink, yellow or green, all of which had been purchased in Bond Street for their French visit.

Instead, she had found in her mother's trunk a gown of pale mauve gauze which had chiffon softly draped round the *décolletage* and small sleeves, which made it seem less formal than some of the others.

It was a gown which after buying it Lady Waltham had complained was too young for her.

But because it was her favourite colour she had sometimes put it on to dine alone with her husband and daughter but had not considered it elaborate enough for any other occasion.

There was a long wrap of the same colour but in velvet to wear with it, and it was in fact one of the few evening-wraps that had not been edged or lined with fur and had therefore escaped being sold.

It was so long since Vernita had worn evening-dress that when she tried to see herself in the small cracked mirror that hung on the wall in the attic she had been pleased with her appearance.

She felt as if, like Cinderella, her Godmother had waved a magic-wand and her rags had turned into a Ball-gown.

Now she was half-afraid that the Count would be ashamed to be seen with her and she looked up at him, her eyes wide and anxious as he reached her side.

Taking her hand, he raised it to his lips.

"You are not only punctual," he said, "which is unusual for one of your sex, but you look very lovely."

The words, Vernita told herself, meant less in French than they would have in English.

Nevertheless she blushed and found it difficult to reply.

The Count led her across the pavement and helped her into the carriage and when they drove off Vernita could not help a little thrill of excitement at being able to lean back against soft cushions with a rug over her knees.

"I have planned to take you somewhere very quiet where we can talk," the Count said, "but perhaps you would have enjoyed one of the more fashionable Restaurants where 'one can see and be seen'?"

"No, no, of course not," Vernita said quickly, "and I am sure it would be wrong for you to be seen with me."

"Not as far as I am concerned," the Count answered, "but you might receive a lot of invitations which you would find embarrassing to refuse."

She realised he was paying her a compliment and she said after a moment:

"It is very ... exciting for me to go anywhere ... and I have never dined at a ... Restaurant in Paris."

She knew that her mother would have thought it vulgar to eat anywhere except in their own house or those of friends.

As if the Count knew what she was thinking he said:

"As I am a bachelor, you could not come to the house where I am staying. So as I wished to talk to you alone, there is no alternative for us but to visit a Restaurant."

"No, of course not," Vernita agreed.

But she could not help thinking of the cheap,

common places which Louise Danjou was always asking her to visit, and she felt glad that she had never been tempted to accept her suggestions.

The carriage stopped in a small Square with flowering shrubs in the centre of it and a number of striped awnings which proclaimed the presence of small, discreet Restaurants beneath tall, well-built houses.

The footman helped Vernita out of the carriage and she found herself in a Restaurant which was very different from what she had anticipated.

Instead of a vast room filled with tables, which was what she expected, there were several small rooms opening off of one another with velvet sofas round the walls and only a few tables in each room.

There were pictures and mirrors on the walls, and flowers which scented the air.

A *Madame* in rustling black welcomed them and led them to a sofa-table that was situated at the end of the room and seemed to be isolated from the others.

Vernita sat down and large menus encased in red leather were placed in front of them both.

Vernita looked at hers helplessly. There were so many dishes to choose from and she had almost forgotten what the names described.

"I know you are hungry," the Count said, "and I am therefore going to order for you. It is always a mistake when you have eaten very little for a long time to have heavy dishes which are difficult to digest."

Vernita was thankful that she had to do nothing but listen to him ordering carefully what seemed to her to be a very large meal.

Then he chose the wine and sat back comfortably, turning sideways so that he could look at her.

"Your first dinner in a Restaurant," he said, "and I have a feeling it is the first time you have ever dined alone with a man who was not your father."

"Y-yes," she replied. "That is true."

"Then I am very honoured to be the first. We must make it a very special occasion, especially as it is something which will not happen again."

"When are you leaving?" she asked.

"I honestly do not know," the Count replied, "but we both know we have to make the most of this evening, then perhaps forget that it ever happened."

Vernita felt a little pang within her that she could not understand, but it was definitely a physical pain.

After tonight, she told herself, she would be just a servant in the Hôtel de Charost, where the Count would speak to her only to give an order, and there would be no question of their being friends as she felt they were at the moment.

"Forget tomorrow," the Count said as if he once again knew what she was thinking, "and let us enjoy every moment of the present. Tell me what interests you."

Making an effort to fall in with the mood he was trying to create, Vernita replied:

"Reading, when I can find the books, and riding when I have a horse."

"I should have guessed both those things," the Count said. "What else?"

Vernita made a little gesture with her hand.

"I used to play the piano a little, but I am sadly out of practice. I am afraid I have never had an aptitude for water-colours like most of my friends."

As she spoke she wondered if she had made a slip.

While all English girls were encouraged to sketch or to paint, she had no idea if their French counterparts were expected to do the same.

Hurriedly she added:

"I was admiring the horses you drive."

"Alas, they are not mine," the Count replied. "They belong to *Vicomte* de Cleremont, a friend who has lent them to me. I am staying in his house in the Champs Élysées."

"Oh, I know the Hôtel de Cleremont!" Vernita exclaimed. "I have often admired the coat of arms on the portico."

"My friend the *Vicomte* admires it too," the Count said, smiling. "As you doubtless know, he belongs to a very ancient family who were related to the Emperor Charlemagne."

Feeling that the Count might expect her to know more about the old families of France than she did, Vernita changed the subject.

"I have always heard that Sweden is a very beautiful country."

"I think so myself, but then I am prejudiced," the Count replied. "I would love you to see the horses I myself own. I have several which I believe are unequalled."

"I had a horse of my own," Vernita said, "and I loved him more than anything else in the world except for my parents. I taught him to come when I whistled, and although he was very spirited with everyone else he would do whatever I asked of him."

"What was his name?" the Count asked.

"Dragonfly," Vernita replied without thinking, and then realised she had said the word in English.

For a moment her heart stood still in sheer terror at the mistake she had made.

She had in fact been so carried away that she had imagined herself back at home standing at the gate of the paddock, giving a short whistle and knowing that Dragonfly as soon as he heard it would come trotting up to her.

"So your horse had an English name," the Count remarked.

"He came from England," Vernita said quickly. "My father bought him when the Armistice was signed."

Even as she spoke she thought it was rather a lame excuse. After all, that would have given her a very short time in which to own the horse and to train him, but she hoped the Count would not realise that.

Fortunately at that moment the waiter brought the wine to the table in a bucket of ice and opened the bottle.

The Count tasted it, nodded his head and the waiter poured out a glass for Vernita.

She looked at it doubtfully.

"It is such a long time since I have had anything alcoholic to drink," she said, "that I think perhaps it would be a mistake."

"It would be until you have eaten," the Count agreed, "and then I promise I will look after you and not allow you to drink too much."

There was a note in his voice that made her feel shy and because she did not dare to look at him she broke the roll that was on her plate and spread it with a small piece of butter.

The roll was fresh and because she was hungry she thought that it was delicious.

But to her surprise the Count leaned across and took the plate away from her.

"I do not wish you to blunt your appetite until you see what I have ordered," he said. "The food here is delicious. It is one of the small places in Paris which cater for the *gourmet* and that is what you are to be tonight."

Vernita smiled.

"I am hungry and it is hard to wait."

"I know that," he answered, "but I know too that you will find it difficult not to gobble up the first thing that comes. Then because you have been without food for so long it would be impossible to eat any more."

"How do you know this?" Vernita questioned.

"I have been hungry—very hungry at times," the Count answered.

"Have you? But when?" Vernita asked in surprise.

"When I have been travelling," he replied, but she felt somehow that that was not entirely a truthful answer.

When the food arrived it was so delicious that

as the Count had predicted Vernita ate every morsel of the first course, then found it impossible to eat more than a few mouthfuls of the second.

"You will disappoint the *Monsieur* who owns this Restaurant and who is also the Chef," the Count said to Vernita, but it was no use.

The months of privation prevented her from doing justice to the dish and finally she admitted that she was defeated and the Count ate alone.

Finally when the waiter had brought their coffee he said:

"Now I am going to talk to you about yourself, Vernita."

She looked at him in surprise because he had used her Christian name, but she did not speak and he went on:

"I am worried as to what will happen to you in the future, and I can only beg you to be very careful, very careful indeed, not to get embroiled in a position from which you cannot extricate yourself."

"I do not ... think I quite ... understand what you mean," Vernita answered.

"How old are you?"

"I am nineteen. I shall be twenty in two months' time."

"Your father died how many years ago?"

"Two."

"Since then you have been living alone with your mother?"

"Yes."

"I cannot understand what happened to the friends you must have had when your father was alive."

Vernita's eye-lashes were very dark against her pale cheeks.

"Mama ... was ill," she said in a hesitating voice, "and as we were ... so poor we could not ... entertain ... and could hardly expect people ... to entertain us."

"I suppose I understand," the Count said, "but it seems strange that two people so attractive as you

and your mother should not have had dozens of
friends wishing to stand by you once you had run into trouble."

"Perhaps we were too . . . proud to want . . . char-
ity," Vernita said, trying to find a plausible explanation.

"As I see friendship," the Count said, "it is being
fond of people whatever their circumstances, whatever happens, and most of all standing by them
when they are in difficulties."

It was what Vernita thought herself and she said
impulsively:

"That of course is what we all feel we should
do . . . but human nature is very frail."

"Is that what you have found?"

"No, I have found kindness . . . like yours," Vernita
said.

She spoke without thinking, then thought it
sounded forward, and she blushed.

"Thank you," the Count answered quietly. "I
want to help you, Vernita, I want to desperately, but
I am not really sure how to go about it."

He made a sound that was like a deep sigh, before he said:

"I am only in Paris as a bird of passage. As I
have told you already, I may have to leave at any
moment. I am not certain if I have done the right
thing in taking you to the Hôtel de Charost."

"It will be much better than being . . . alone without . . . Mama."

"That is what I thought until I saw you this morning."

"Did I do anything wrong?" Vernita asked.

"Not wrong," the Count answered. "I thought
when I saw you yesterday that you were not the
seamstress you professed to be, but I was sorry for
you and realised that you were on the borderline of
starvation. However, this morning . . ."

He paused a moment, then he went on:

"When I saw you in your mauve gown I knew
that what I had suspected was true. You were a lady

and born to a very different life from the one you are
now living."

"Being well-bred does not prevent one from feeling hungry," Vernita smiled, "and I doubt if my
family-tree would bring me in one extra *sou* when it
comes to earning my own living."

"It is fortunate that you can sew so well."

"My mother embroidered beautifully, and she
could also do tapestry-work. It was the one saleable
talent we had."

There was a note almost of despair in her voice
as she remembered that however talented they were
it had not saved her mother from dying.

"I am worried," the Count said.

"About what?"

"About you. What will become of you? What will
happen to you next year and the year after that?"

Vernita longed to reply that the only thing
which could help her would be the end of the war,
but instead she said:

"Perhaps the Princess will find me indispensable
and I shall be able to travel with her."

"Why should you say that?" the Count asked.

"I know she has only recently returned from
Rome," Vernita answered, "and presumably, as it is
her husband's country and he owns such vast estates
there, one day she will return."

"I imagine so," the Count replied, "but it does
not reassure me in any way to think of you sur-
rounded by Italians who, although they may be fascinating to most women, are very unreliable."

Quite so suddenly that Vernita was startled, he
brought his fist down hard on the table so that the
coffee-cups rattled.

"*Nom de Dieu!*" he swore. "You must know what
I am trying to say. How in the life you have chosen
and for which there seems to be no alternative are
you ever to find yourself a husband?"

"A . . . husband?" Vernita asked in surprise.

"That, surely, is the goal of all young women,

and marriage is something you will be forced to
consider for yourself if there is no-one else to do it
for you."

"It has been . . . impossible for me to think of . . .
marriage," Vernita said in a low voice.

"But you need love, like everyone else, and the
love you will be offered in the Hôtel de Charost will
not include a wedding-ring."

Vernita looked astonished; then, half-turning her
face away from the Count, she said:

"D-do you . . . do you mean . . . ?"

"Of course that is what I mean!" the Count interrupted sharply. "You are very beautiful and the
Hôtel de Charost is always full of men, men who
come to see the Princess, but when they set eyes on
you they will undoubtedly look and look again."

He paused before he went on:

"Besides that, there is the household itself, the
Chamberlain, the Chief Equerry, besides a whole
number of other men who unless they are blind will
certainly try to make love to you, and I have a feeling you will not know how to refuse their advances
even if you should wish to do so."

"You are . . . frightening . . . me!"

"I want to frighten you," the Count replied. "I
want you to realise what lies in front of you and to be
prepared! *Mon Dieu!* But I wish there was somewhere else I could take you!"

Vernita was still for a moment, then she said:

"I . . . understand what you are saying to me, and
I know you are trying to do what is . . . best for me . . .
but what I think you are . . . forgetting is that I know
in my heart what is . . . right and wrong, and I would
never do . . . anything of which my father and mother
would not have approved."

The Count smiled and it swept the grimness
from his face.

"Do you suppose I do not know that?" he asked.
"Your beauty and your innocence, Vernita, surround
you like a light. Unfortunately, it can also, in this

city, prove an irresistible attraction to a large number
of men who are satiated with women who have long
forgotten what such words mean."

Vernita thought for a moment, then almost as if
she spoke the words without conscious volition she
said very quietly:

"When you leave...could you not...take me
with you?"

She did not actually mean what the words implied.

She merely thought that if he was returning to
Sweden, perhaps from there she could escape to
England and to her home, which would still be
waiting for her even if her father and mother were
no longer alive.

But the Count, looking at her incredulously, answered, and his voice was raw:

"Do you suppose that is not what I want? What
I would wish to do if I had the choice? But it is
impossible! There are reasons which I cannot explain
why I must not become involved with you."

The way he spoke as well as the words he used
surprised her.

She looked at him wide-eyed and found there
was an expression on his face which held her and
made it impossible for her to look away.

For a long, long moment they sat looking at
each other, then the Count said:

"This is madness for us both! I will take you
home."

He called for the bill while Vernita sat feeling as
if the world had turned upside-down and she had no
idea what to do about it. It was impossible to think
straight and her mind was chaotic.

All she knew was that her heart was beating
frantically in her breast and she felt as if the Count
was moving away from her into a misty distance.

She wanted more than she had ever wanted anything in her whole life to hold on to him and prevent
him from going.

The bill was paid and the *Madame* bowed them
out onto the street were the carriage was waiting.

They got into it and Vernita thought that the Count deliberately sat as far away from her as possible.

As the horses moved off she glanced at him from under her eye-lashes and saw that his face was set sternly, the cynical lines on each side of his mouth deeply etched.

He was staring straight ahead and she thought despairingly that he was not only upset but also angry with her.

In a small voice that was so low he could hardly hear it she said:

"If . . . I have upset you . . . I did not mean to do so . . . it has been such a . . . wonderful evening for me . . . and I have been . . . happy, very happy . . . until you were . . . angry."

"I am not angry—not with you," the Count replied.

Then as he turned to look at her, her face shadowy in the gathering dusk outside, he gave a sudden exclamation that was almost a groan, and putting out his arms pulled her roughly against him.

He did not speak, he only tipped her head back against his shoulder, then his lips were on hers.

For a moment Vernita was too surprised, too astonished, even to realise what was happening.

Then as she found it difficult to breathe, and his lips, hard and compelling, seemed to take possession of her, she felt a sensation that was warm and wonderful move from her breast up through her body until it reached her lips.

It was then that she knew that the first kiss she had ever received was different from what she had expected.

It was so marvellous, so ecstatic, that she felt as if she floated in the air and the Count carried her up into the sky.

She felt as if her whole body responded to him and pulsated with a thousand strange emotions she had never known existed.

His arms tightened round her.

Her lips were soft and yielding and his became more demanding, more insistent, until it seemed to Vernita that they both vibrated to a music which filled the air and yet came from their hearts.

When finally the Count raised his head she quivered against him, but it was not with fear but with a rapture she had never known before in her whole life.

"What have you done to me, Vernita?" he asked. "Oh, my little love, I have fought against behaving like this, but you were too much for me."

There was a deep note in his voice which made her feel shy.

She turned her face to hide it against his shoulder, but he put his fingers under her chin and forced it upwards so that he could look down into her eyes.

"I lay awake all night and told myself that if I was wise and sensible I would leave you alone," he said, "but it was impossible."

"Why?" Vernita whispered.

"Because I want you," he replied. "Because you attract me as no woman has ever done before, and because already your sweet face and your violet eyes are haunting me."

As he spoke his lips were on hers and he was kissing her again, kissing her frantically and passionately.

It was as if he felt he was losing her and must make her his.

Now it seemed to Vernita as if there were little flames of fire rising from her toes up through her body until they reached her lips and touched the fire that she sensed in him.

It was so rapturous, so perfect, that she thought she must be imagining the wonder of it and it could not be real.

And yet she felt that her whole body pulsated with the fire he had ignited in her which she did not understand. She only knew she longed for him to hold her even closer and go on kissing her.

Then almost as roughly as he had pulled her into his arms the Count set her free.

"I am behaving abominably!" he said. "This
should never have happened! I am ashamed of myself, but, my darling, you drive me crazy!"

"Does it . . . matter?" Vernita asked.

"I am trying to think of you," the Count said
despairingly.

"I love . . . you!"

She thought even as she spoke that it was not for
her to say the words, and yet they came to her lips
and seemed as natural as breathing.

She knew this was love and it was a light that
invaded her body.

It was there, vivid, beautiful, and pure—it came
from Heaven itself and was a part of her prayers
which could not be denied.

Gently now the Count put out his arms and drew
her to him again.

"You must not love me," he said. "You must forget me. I will go away. I will leave at once."

"No . . . please . . . please do not do that," Vernita
cried. "I love you . . . I love you as I never thought it
possible to . . . love . . . anybody. I had no idea that
. . . love was like . . . this."

"Like what?" the Count asked.

"So glorious . . . so wonderful . . . like being close
to . . . God."

She spoke in an ecstatic voice which although it
was very low seemed to vibrate round the carriage.
The Count gave a groan and held her close against
him, his lips on her hair.

"My precious, my sweet darling," he said, "this
should never have happened to us."

"But it has!" Vernita cried. "I think the first moment I saw you I knew that you were . . . different
from any . . . man I had ever seen . . . before. Then
when you were so kind to me I somehow felt as if it
was . . . meant that you should be there in my life."

"It may have been meant in the Great Pattern of

things," the Count said, "something in our Karma
which was planned so that when we met we would
recognise each other. But not now—not at this moment."

"But why?" Vernita asked. "I do not understand."

"I cannot explain," the Count replied. "All I
know is that I wanted to help you the moment I first
set eyes on you, but I did not mean anything else
to happen! Now I must go away and we must make
ourselves forget each other."

"How . . . can I do . . . that?" Vernita asked.

Then as if what he was saying sank fully into her
consciousness she gave a little cry of horror and
pressed herself closely to him, her hand holding on to
the lapel of his coat.

"Do not leave me . . . please do not leave me!" she
begged. "I know . . . even though you say it is . . .
wrong . . . that . . . God brought us . . . together."

She gave a little sob before she went on:

"I was so lonely . . . so unhappy . . . so utterly and
completely miserable . . . but now everything is wonderful. I have been taken up from the darkness of
Hell into Heaven itself. I love you! I love you with
. . . all of me . . . and . . . nothing can change that."

"My darling, my precious!" the Count said bro-
kenly. "I am not worthy of your love. It is something
perfect that I never expected to find, not at any rate
in Paris."

"We have found it," Vernita persisted, "and
whether it is right or wrong it has . . . happened, and
nothing we can say or do can take that . . . away from
us."

She felt the Count's arms tighten, then his lips
were on her forehead, kissing the smooth oval with a
gentleness which made tears come into her eyes.

"Please do not go away," she pleaded. "If you
do I shall want only to . . . die, as Mama has . . . died.
I know that if . . . you are not . . . there I shall have no
wish to go on . . . living."

"You must not say such things," he said sternly.

"They are true," Vernita insisted. "In the past I always thought love was something quiet and soft and romantic, like the moonlight and the scent of roses. But what I feel for you is so . . . intense that it is an . . . ecstasy beyond words. It is also a . . . pain which seems to be . . . tearing me apart."

"What do you think I am feeling?" the Count asked.

Then he was kissing her again—kissing her until it was impossible to think, but only to know that they were enveloped in a light and a glory so wonderful, so miraculous, that Vernita knew she could never be the same again.

The horse drew to a standstill and almost as if they came back from another world Vernita slowly drew herself from the Count's arms and waited for the footman to open the door.

"You must leave me," the Count said, "because, my darling heart, I do not think I can bear any more."

"I shall . . . see you . . . tomorrow?" Vernita asked, and there was a fear beneath the words that he could hear in her voice.

"I shall see you tomorrow," he answered. "I will fetch you in the morning and take you to the Hôtel de Charost."

"And you will not . . . leave Paris without . . . telling me?"

"I swear to you that I will not do that. I am not even certain that I can bear to go, even though it is what I know I should do."

"Please . . . stay."

He was unable to answer her because the footman opened the door.

Slowly, because she felt she was losing something so precious, so wonderful, that she would never find it again, Vernita alighted from the carriage.

The Count followed her and pushed open the door of the house, which was not yet locked and barred as it would be later when all the tenants were home.

It seemed to Vernita that it was a century since she last left the ugly Hall with its smell of food.

She did not go into the house but stood in the doorway and held out her hand.

The Count held it for a moment in both of his, but he did not kiss it as he had done when he fetched her. Instead he looked into her eyes and said quietly in a voice which yet seemed to be a cry of despair:

"Good night, my love—my only love."

He turned away and because she could not bear to see him go Vernita closed the door and started to climb the stairs.

Chapter Four

Napoleon was shaving.

Most men entrusted this operation to a valet or a barber, but Napoleon always shaved himself.

Rustam, his Mameluke bodyguard, held a looking-glass while Napoleon lathered his face with soap scented with herbs; then, using a razor that had been immersed in hot water, he shaved with downward movements.

He always bought his razors with mother-of-pearl handles from England because Birmingham steel was superior to the French.

During the Armistice he had purchased some new ones and he thought with satisfaction how closely they removed any sign of a beard.

He had already spent an hour in his bath, for his mother had brought up all her children to be very particular about personal cleanliness.

After his bath but before he cleaned his teeth Napoleon had washed his hands with almond-paste and his face, neck, and ears with a sponge and soap.

He had excellent teeth, naturally white and strong, which never required the attention of his dentist, who therefore received six thousand *francs* a year for doing practically nothing.

His shaving finished, Napoleon's second valet, Constant, poured *Eau de Cologne* over his head and as it trickled down his bare torso Napoleon frictioned his arms and chest with a hard-bristled brush while the valet did the same to his shoulders and back.

"Your sister is behaving badly as usual," a voice said from the other side of the room.

Napoleon turned his head to where his wife, Joséphine, was sitting watching him.

He thought vaguely as he did so that she was looking attractive. He was still very fond of her. To him she was still the pretty, *petite* widow he had been so wildly in love with that she had almost broken his heart with her infidelities.

Joséphine's silky light-chestnut hair had lost some of its colour, but her dazzling white skin and her pretty voice with its light, creole accent were unchanged.

Her weak feature had always been her teeth, so that when she laughed she was careful barely to part her lips, making the laughter bubble in her throat.

"Are you talking about Paulina?" Napoleon asked sharply.

"Of course! Who else?"

Napoleon put on his fine linen shirt before he answered.

"What has Paulina done now?"

He knew that his wife and his favourite sister hated each other and he was always wary about the stories of Paulina's indiscretions which Joséphine repeated to him all too eagerly.

It was not in fact surprising that Joséphine should dislike not only Paulina but the rest of the Bonaparte family.

They had all been unpleasant to her when she was first married to Napoleon and had spent their time since in trying to make trouble between husband and wife.

She was well aware they were always hinting that he should divorce her so that he could have a son.

Joséphine unfortunately had had an accident in Plombières when Napoleon was in Egypt.

A balcony on which she was standing had collapsed and she had fallen fifteen feet. The internal injuries she suffered meant she would never have another child.

Now that he was Emperor, the spectre of Napoleon getting rid of her hovered over her like a menacing cloud.

She was not only afraid of being divorced, she was also in love with her husband, which she had certainly not been when they were first married.

Sometimes when she was honest with herself, Joséphine, remembering the passionate letters that Napoleon had written to her during the Italian Campaign at a time when she was with a lover, admitted it was poetic justice.

She would take out his letters and read the words he had written in the first months of their marriage.

No letters from you! I get one only every four days, whereas if you loved me you would write twice a day. . . . I love you more each day! Absence cures small passions but increases great ones.

"How could I have been so foolish?" she asked herself, and would pick up another in which Napoleon had written:

My tears drop on your portrait. It alone is always with me.

Aloud she said now:

"Paulina has a new lover. Already everybody is beginning to talk about the indiscreet way in which she is behaving with him, and he is always at the Hôtel de Charost."

"Who is he?" Napoleon asked abruptly.

His valet was helping him into the frock-coat he preferred. Simple, without lace and embroidery, it had a scarlet collar and scarlet edges to the lapels.

Now he took from his valet a handkerchief sprinkled with *Eau de Cologne* which he put into his right-hand pocket and a snuff-box which he slipped into his left.

"He is called Count Axel de Storvik," Joséphine replied. "He is a Swede and is trying to sell a new gun which he says will out-distance anything you are using at the moment."

"I have heard of him," Napoleon remarked briefly.

"Then buy his gun and tell him to leave your sister alone. She should be concerning herself with her husband and not with some Swede who will give her a worse name than she has already."

"I will tell Fouché to make enquiries about him," Napoleon said as he walked towards the door.

He left the room and Joséphine knew that she would not see him again until dinner-time, when he ate with her and friends at about seven-thirty.

Napoleon had two meals a day; his luncheon was at eleven o'clock, which he ate alone at a small mahogany pedestal-table while he was still working.

He ate quickly and liked simple food. He drank an inexpensive red Burgundy with his meals and consumed about a half-bottle a day diluted with water.

When he had gone Joséphine sighed, and at the same time she thought that she had got her own back on her sister-in-law, for past insults.

She had not forgotten nor forgiven the way that Paulina and her sisters had behaved before the Coronation last December.

Napoleon had been undecided as to whether Josèphine was to be crowned as Empress.

The whole family had attacked her, trying to convince Napoleon that now was the time to divorce her, throwing at him all her infidelities and extravagances.

Joséphine had collapsed, weeping and distraught.

But when Napoleon saw his sisters exchanging triumphant looks he had comforted his wife and supported her against his squabbling, vindictive family.

The new Princesses, Carolina, Elisa, and Pau-

lina, had then united in a spiteful trick against the
new Empress at the Ceremony in the Cathedral.

After Joséphine had risen from her knees to
move back to the throne with the crown on her head,
the three Bonaparte sisters allowed the full weight
of her ermine-lined velvet train to fall against her,
with the result that she almost stumbled as she
mounted the steps of the dais.

Fortunately, Napoleon's eagle-eye saw what was
happening and he hissed a low but effective warning
so that his sisters quickly picked up Joséphine's train
again.

Joséphine would never forget that moment, any
more than Paulina could forget an occasion when her
sister-in-law had been the victor.

She and Prince Camillo Borghese were to pay a
formal visit to Joséphine soon after their Civil Wedding.

Paulina was in a triumphant mood, pleased with
Prince Camillo's wealth and importance. She thought
she would impress Joséphine and make her jealous
by a parade of dazzling jewellery in addition to her
new title.

She knew her beauty could easily outweigh that
of Joséphine, who had turned forty, and her fashionable, light, almost transparent draperies suited Paulina to perfection.

Covered with diamonds, she and Prince Camillo
Borghese arrived at the Palace of St. Cloud in a six-
horse carriage with liveried out-riders. They were announced by a Chamberlain in stentorian tones.

Paulina was wearing green, a gown she had chosen with great care, and only as she advanced into the
Reception-Room did she realise it was furnished and
draped entirely in blue.

At the far end of it sat Joséphine in a simple
gown of white muslin with no ornamentation of any
sort save a golden girdle.

Her spies had informed her what her sister-in-
law would be wearing, and she made her look foolish as only a clever woman could.

Paulina had seethed with mortification and in-
ward fury, but the two women had kissed each other
as if there were no venom in their hearts.

Going now to her own bed-room, Joséphine
thought with delight that once again she was striking
a blow at the woman she hated because she held
such a very important place in Napoleon's heart.

If anyone could find out anything to her and the
Swede's disadvantage it would be Fouché, the fer-
rety, unpleasant Minister of Police.

Everybody in Paris was terrified of him and he
was no favourite of Napoleon except that he had his
uses.

"Fouché will certainly discover what is happening," Joséphine told herself, "and then Napoleon will
force Paulina to behave herself."

The Emperor was in fact thinking the same
thing as he sat down at his desk. It was two minutes
past nine and he was therefore two minutes late.

As usual there was a great pile of papers for him
to attend to and a crowd waiting in the Ante-Room
for an audience.

Yet as he opened the first paper which lay on the
desk in front of him, his mind was for the moment
still on Paulina.

*　*　*

It was late in the afternoon and Paulina was beginning to dress for the evening.

Vernita had found that almost the whole day was
spent by Paulina in preparing herself for what was
more or less a public appearance when she attended
the Receptions, the Balls, or the parties to which she
was invited in the evening.

During the afternoon Vernita knew the Princess
had received a number of her intimate friends in the
Grand Salon decorated in poppy-red velvet which
was a perfect background for her dark hair.

Now, sitting in front of her mirror, she was looking with critical eyes at the clearness of her skin,
while her lady's-maid brought from her wardrobe a

number of gowns so that she could decide what she would wear that evening.

Vernita had been sent for to repair the hem on a gown of pale green gauze that glittered with tiny sequins of gold and at the same time had a Grecian look in the draperies round the very low *décolletage*.

"I might wear that," Paulina said reflectively, "and my hair can be arranged in ringlets with gold ribbons and cameo brooches."

Then she said:

"But perhaps I may meet someone tonight who has seen me wearing it before, and that would be a mistake."

She turned round from the mirror to look at the other gowns, one in white and pink, the other in pale jonquil yellow which sparkled with topazes.

"I am tired of those," she said petulantly. "Bring me some others."

The maids hurried to obey while Vernita knelt on the floor, still repairing the green gown as she had been told to do.

Princess Paulina glanced at her as if she saw her for the first time.

"You sew well," she said. "Do you like being here?"

"I am very grateful to Your Imperial Highness for employing me," Vernita answered.

She had felt lonely and frightened when she arrived. But the servants had been kinder than she had expected and she liked the small room she had been given high up at the top of the house.

It overlooked the garden at the far end of which was a wall bordering on the Champs Élysés. She thought of the Count living there and felt that somehow she was nearer to him.

She had been unable to sleep the night before because of the wonder he had evoked in her and the happiness that seemed to make her whole body vibrate with ecstasy.

She did not feel as she had felt alone in the dingy attic which had been her home for two years, but was caught up in a celestial glory, enveloped with clouds of happiness, and diffused with a light that was not of this world.

Only when the morning came did she remember that today she had to go to the Hôtel de Charost and take up her duties as a servant. It might be hard, very hard, for the Count even to speak to her, let alone touch her again.

She longed as she had never longed for anything in her whole life to be in his arms, to feel his lips on hers, and to know that he evoked in her a rapture, a love that she had never thought or dreamt she would ever know.

It seemed incredible that within such a short space of time she should have found the man she loved and who had told her that he loved her too.

"Thank you, God, thank you!" she whispered in the darkness.

She thought perhaps in some strange way it was her mother who had brought the Count to her and had swept away the misery and loneliness that she would have been feeling had he not come into her life.

"Take care of him, Mama," Vernita prayed, "and please let him stay with me. Do not let him go away. How can I . . . lose him . . . now?"

There was a little sob in the last words, but even so she was too happy to cry.

She had found what she was seeking. She had found love when she least expected it, and no-one, she told herself, could be more wonderful than the Count.

She dressed early and finished her packing, said good-bye to *Madame* Danjou and Louise, who were going out shopping, and then persuaded *Monsieur* to carry her trunks down the stairs.

He grumbled because they were heavy. Vernita had not listened to what he was saying but had stood at the door, looking out into the street, waiting for the Count's horses to appear.

But when the carriage arrived it was emblazoned

with the coat of arms of the Princess and there was
no-one inside it.

She felt as disappointed as a child who had been
promised a treat that was cancelled at the last moment.

"The Chamberlain of Her Imperial Highness has
sent a carriage for you, *M'mselle*," the footman said,
"and I was to tell you that if you wish to stop and
buy materials at one of the shops on the way back to
the Hôtel de Charost we'll wait for you."

Vernita was sure that this arrangement had been
made by the Count and that he was thinking of her
and saving her from going alone to the shops.

At the same time, she was terrified in case this
meant that he was planning to leave Paris and she
would not see him again.

However, she learnt later, when she arrived at
the Hôtel de Charost, that the Princess had gone
driving with the Count in the Bois and she understood that this was why he had been prevented from
collecting her himself as he had promised.

She was tactful and sensible enough to make
herself pleasant to the older housemaids and other
servants in the household.

She was well aware how even at her old home
the old-stagers had always resented the advent of
someone new, and she was very humble and con-
ciliatory in order to make a good impression.

"I am very anxious to please Her Imperial Highness," she said to the lady's-maids, "and I should be
very grateful if you would help me not to make mis-
takes or do anything that is wrong."

Their hostility disappeared and when they had
luncheon she knew from the way they gossipped in
front of her and explained who they were talking
about that they accepted her as one of themselves.

"It is impossible for anyone in Paris, or anywhere
in the world for that matter, to be as beautiful as our
mistress," one of the Princess's lady's-maids said en
thusiastically.

"She's difficult, though," the other said. "She was

in a devil's mood when she came to bed at two o'clock this morning."

"What happened?" the other one asked.

"One of those old Dowagers of the *ancien régime* got their claws into her, I imagine. You know she's sensitive like the rest of her family because after all they're Corsicans and not French."

Vernita was surprised that the servants should speak so frankly, but she was well aware that everything that happened in a household was always known to the staff. Her father had said often enough with a twinkle in his eye:

"No man is a hero to his valet and I doubt if any woman is a beauty to her lady's-maid!"

The Princess's lady's-maids told Vernita how their mistress had to hide her ears as they were the one defect in her otherwise perfect body.

"She even covered one ear with her hand," the maid went on, "when in Rome she was carved in marble by Canova, who's supposed to be the greatest sculptor in Italy."

"Ears or no ears," the other maid answered, "it's not surprising that men fall in love with her."

"And her with them!" the other maid added.

They both laughed rather unkindly, Vernita thought.

As the Princess was out, the lady's-maids offered to show her the house and she was entranced with the brilliance of the colours the Princess had chosen when she had redecorated the whole Mansion.

The Duke de Charost had been a tutor to the young Louise XVI and his widow had been paid 400,000 *francs* by the Princess Paulina for the Hôtel de Charost.

She had then cleared out the elegant eighteenth-century furniture and replaced it with what was considered to be fashionable and up-to-date at the moment and had painted the rooms with the flamboyant colours that she and her brother preferred.

The *Salon Ionian* was hung with draped poppy-coloured velvet fringed with gold. The *Chambre de*

Parade was a brilliant blue and the Library was orange.

All the time the maids were taking Vernita round the house, they chattered.

They told her how angry one of the kitchen-maids was because she had been told that she had to marry Paul the Negro and they related how when the Princess felt cold in the winter she often warmed her feet on the *décolletage* of a lady-in-waiting who was told to lie on the floor!

Vernita at first had thought they must be joking, but she was beginning to realise that the Princess was a law unto herself.

She found the Charost Chapel had been converted into a Billiard-Room papered in yellow and silver, and that the religious pictures had been taken away and hung in the room used by the valets.

Long before the tour was finished Vernita was longing to laugh at some of the things she had been told and wanted to relate to the Count all she had heard.

Only he, she thought, would understand how funny it all was and perhaps would feel as she did— that it was not surprising that what was left of the aristocratic French families looked askance at the behaviour of the Bonapartes and resented seeing them in positions of importance.

The day, apart from Vernita's tour of the house, seemed to pass slowly because she was longing with an intensity which almost frightened her to see the Count again.

Supposing she should learn later in the evening that he had gone away, as he had said he might have to do?

Then she remembered that he had promised her that he would let her know if he was leaving, and she knew that if it was humanly possible he would keep his word.

She could not help wondering what was the reason for his being so determined that their love could mean nothing and they must try to forget each other.

She was well aware that in his eyes she was of no importance—a penniless Frenchwoman without a social background.

But even if he was not prepared to marry her, she could not understand why, if he loved her, they could not meet each other, could not be together secretly, even if he must not be seen with her in public.

It was all very puzzling, and at the same time Vernita was wondering whether she was brave enough to tell him the truth about herself.

She knew he would not denounce her to the Police since after all he was not French but Swedish.

But at the same time she thought perhaps the mere fact that she was an enemy of the Bonapartes and indeed of the whole country might, if it was ever discovered, cause damage to the man she loved.

One thing she told herself she must never do was to harm him by putting him in a position where he might be accused of harbouring one of the hated English.

"It would be a mistake to tell him who I am," Vernita decided finally.

At the same time, she longed to be frank and open and to tell the Count she was not the starving nonentity he thought her to be, but someone who could hold her head high in any society, especially in the pseudo-grand, upstart Empire of the Bonapartes.

The maids came back to Paulina with more gowns, one of white gauze which sparkled with diamanté and another of very pale green which was decorated with pink almond-blossoms.

Paulina looked at them and exclaimed:

"I have just remembered! I was wearing my diamond ear-rings which go with that white gown yesterday afternoon and I have left one of them by the State Bed downstairs."

She turned to Vernita and said:

"Run down and bring it back to me. It is on the bed-side table. I remembered to put on one when I rose from the bed and forgot the other."

She turned to the mirror as she finished speaking and Vernita intercepted a glance that passed between the two lady's-maids.

She knew by the expressions on their faces exactly what they were thinking.

She felt a sudden pang of jealousy drive into her breast like a dagger.

Was it the Count, she wondered, for whom the Princess had removed her ear-rings as she lay in the State Bed under the gold rosettes on the white canopy?

Obediently she rose and put down the gown she was mending to go from the Princess's room down the stairs.

She entered the *Chambre de Parade,* which held the State Bed, and found it enveloped with the light of the setting sun.

Outside the long windows, the flowers were brilliant in the garden and Vernita stood looking out onto the green lawns, the trees vivid against the blue sky.

It made her feel suddenly home-sick for the garden which she and her mother had planned together and beyond the garden the paddocks with the horses standing beneath the trees and swishing their tails.

She was lost for a moment in her thoughts and started as a voice behind her asked:

"Who are you? I do not remember seeing you here before."

She turned round and gave a little exclamation.

There was no need for her to be told who was speaking to her. She immediately recognised the Emperor Napoleon from his pictures and from having seen him once before when she had first come to Paris.

She curtseyed, her eye-lashes dark against her pale skin, and as she rose Napoleon walked across the room to stand beside her.

She knew that he was waiting for an answer to his question and after a moment she replied:

"I am ... employed, Your Majesty, as ... seam-stress to Her Imperial Highness. I only ... arrived to-day."

"That is why your face is unfamiliar," Napoleon said, "and a very pretty face it is too!"

"I thank Your Majesty," Vernita said nervously. "I have been sent to find Her Imperial Highness's ear-ring which she left beside the bed."

Napoleon's expression darkened and Vernita re-alised she had been indiscreet.

She would have moved away but he said:

"What is your name?"

"Vernita ... Bernier, Your Majesty."

"Vernita! A name I have not heard before, but you have violet eyes and if I were choosing a name for you I would call you Violet!"

Vernita looked surprised. She did not know that Napoleon always invented new names for the women he admired.

Joséphine had been known as Rose when he first met her. His first love, Désirée, he called Eugénie, and all through his life he thought of better names for the women who impressed him than the ones by which they had been christened.

"Your eyes are violet," he went on now before Vernita could speak. "The violet is a flower of which I am very fond."

There was a note in his voice which made Vernita know that what he was saying was dangerous and that she must leave him quickly.

"Her Imperial Highness is ... expecting me ... Sire," she said breathlessly.

She would have run from the room without wait-ing for the ear-ring if Napoleon had not put out his arms to stop her.

She was too late and he caught her even as she began to run and pulled her against him.

Vernita realised that he was going to kiss her and frantically she struggled against him, but he was strong.

She was helpless against the strength of his

arms and the expression in his eyes told her that he meant to be the conqueror.

Then, as she turned her head from side to side, knowing it was only a question of seconds before he succeeded in his intention of capturing her lips, a voice from the door said:

"I have been longing to meet Your Majesty, and this is a Heaven-sent opportunity!"

Vernita felt her heart leap with relief, and before Napoleon released her from his grasp she knew who stood there.

"Who are you?"

The Emperor's question was sharp but his arms round Vernita slackened and in a moment she was free of him.

The Count advanced across the room to click his heels and bow his head.

"May I, Sire, present myself?" he asked. "I am Count Axel de Storvik, and I have been hoping for an opportunity to speak with Your Majesty about a matter which is of great military importance!"

As Vernita fled from the room, the Count was speaking with an assurance and a self-confidence which made her feel proud.

She knew that he had deliberately walked into the room to save her and because she knew that he loved her she felt he must have been angry to find her in the Emperor's arms.

A man with less courage might have thought it an intrusion to interrupt the Emperor at such a moment, especially, Vernita thought, as the Count had a personal interest in being in his good graces.

She knew he had acted in her interests and not his own, and she ran up the stairs, her heart still beating frantically and a flush on her cheeks as she told herself that he was so brave and she loved him more than ever.

She entered the bed-room of the Princess Paulina, who, busy at her dressing-table, did not turn her head. Only after a moment, as Vernita did not speak, she asked:

"Did you find the ear-ring?"

"No, Your Imperial Highness. I came back without it because His Majesty the Emperor was downstairs and I thought he must be looking for you."

"The Emperor?" Paulina exclaimed. *"Pardi,* but I did not expect him! I wonder why he has called to see me at this hour?"

For a moment there was a frown between her beautiful eyes. Then she said impatiently to the maids:

"What are you waiting for? Hurry! Bring me my négligée. You have heard that the Emperor is downstairs and will be expecting to see me."

The maids brought a négligée from the wardrobe, and the Princess, who was naked, slipped it on. With a last look at her reflection in the mirror she went from the room and down the stairs.

When she entered the Salon she was surprised to find no-one in it.

Then hearing voices in the next room, which contained the State Bed, she went in to find Count Axel talking to Napoleon.

"You are quite certain it will work," she heard her brother say.

"We have tried it out, Sire, with the most excellent results. In fact I can say quite categorically that there is nothing in Your Majesty's own armoury to equal it."

"Who told you that?" Napoleon asked sharply.

"Marshal Ney, Sire, and General Junot were both convinced that this was an advance on anything that Your Majesty has in the field at the present moment."

Napoleon put his hand to his chin as if he was considering what he had been told, and Paulina ran forward.

"Dearest, I was not expecting you!" she exclaimed, and flung her arms round her brother's neck.

He kissed her and said:

"I came to talk to you alone."

"I will withdraw," the Count said before Paulina

could speak, "but before I do so I would like, Sire, to thank Your Majesty for listening to me."

He bowed his head and without even looking at Paulina turned and walked from the room.

"So Axel has been telling you about his gun," Paulina said to her brother. "He has been itching to do so ever since he came to Paris. *Mon Dieu!* I find guns, muskets, and cannon-balls extremely boring conversation!"

Napoleon laughed.

"I am well aware, my dear sister, of the only topic of conversation that really interests you, and that is what I have come to talk about."

Paulina wrinkled her nose.

"I can guess what you are going to say," she replied. "I suppose it is Joséphine who has suggested that you should speak to me. How I loathe that expression!"

She stamped her foot to emphasize her point and looked at Napoleon from under her eye-lashes to see how he was reacting to what she had said.

With her back to the sunshine she might as well have been naked, and Napoleon looked at her for a moment appraisingly before he said, and his voice was deliberately cold:

"You know as well as I do that you must behave discreetly while Camillo is in Boulogne, otherwise I shall insist upon your returning to Rome."

Paulina threw out her arms and her négligée, insecurely fastened, fell open to reveal her nakedness.

"*Pardi!*" she exclaimed, using as usual her favourite expletive. "But how can I have done anything wrong except breathe? The women, and that includes your ageing, barren wife, are jealous! They have only to see my face to suggest there is something immoral about it."

"At the moment it is not only your face they are complaining about," Napoleon answered.

But now there was a twinkle in his eye and a smile on his lips.

Because she knew he was no longer angry Paulina flung herself against him, her arms round his neck, her cheek against his.

"Oh, dearest Napoleon, why do you listen to them?" she asked. "I have been behaving like an angel—I have really—and if I have done anything of which you would not approve, I swear to you I have locked the door!"

Napoleon laughed again.

"You are hopeless and incorrigible, but I find it hard, my little one, to be angry with you for long!"

Paulina took her arms from round his neck and pulling her négligée round her walked towards the Salon.

"Let us sit on the sofa and talk together," she said. "It is far too long since we have been alone."

"I cannot stay," Napoleon answered. "Tell me about this young Swede I have just met. What does he mean to you?"

"What do you suppose he means?" Paulina asked. "One has to *passer le temps* and after all he is very handsome!"

"I will not have you talked about," Napoleon said. "You know as well as I do that the Courts of Europe are looking at mine with their eye-brows raised. Any hint of scandal is listened to avidly and used as a weapon, as lethal and effective as anything that can be fired at me from a cannon."

He spoke with a touch of bitterness and Paulina put her face against his shoulder in a gesture of affection.

"I will be careful, very, very careful, for your sake, my darling brother."

"I shall be angry with you if you disobey me."

"I promise you I will not only lock the door but also draw down the blinds!"

Napoleon laughed as if he could not help it. Then he rose to say in a different tone of voice:

"There was a very pretty girl here when I arrived. She told me she was your new seamstress."

"Yes, she came today."

Napoleon did not speak and after a moment Paulina said:

"You are interested in her?"

"I may be. She is certainly unusually attractive."

"Is she? I have not really looked at her."

"I might be able to come here tomorrow night via the garden door. Ask her to meet me here."

"I will order her to do so."

"Good!"

Napoleon drew a watch from his waist-coat pocket.

"I have a meeting, then I must return home."

Paulina moved forward to kiss his cheek and with his arm round her they walked towards the door.

"Now behave yourself," he said, "and do not forget to tell little Violet Eyes to be waiting for me at about nine o'clock. I have to attend a dinner, and will leave early."

"I will not forget," Paulina promised.

The Emperor walked across the Hall, passed through the ranks of bowing servants, and got into his carriage that was waiting outside.

Paulina hurried up the stairs.

Nothing could be better, she thought to herself, than that Napoleon should be interested in one of her household.

It would certainly take his mind off her own indiscretions and she was quite certain that it was Joséphine who had put him up to speaking to her about the Count.

"Whatever that woman says," she told herself as she entered her bed-room, "I will not give up Axel, not at any rate for a long time."

She dressed, and when she was ready, looking exceedingly lovely, she sent the lady's-maids from the room, telling Vernita to stay.

There was silence for a moment while Vernita waited rather apprehensively.

She had a feeling that what the Princess Paulina wanted to say to her was somehow connected with her brother.

"The Emperor," Paulina said after a moment, "tells me that you have violet-coloured eyes. Has anyone ever told you that before?"

"N-no, Ma'am," Vernita answered hesitatingly.

She suddenly felt afraid of what the Princess was going to say.

What could the Emperor have told her? Was there a chance of her being dismissed?

"My brother is very fastidious where women are concerned," Paulina went on, looking at her own reflection in the mirror. "It is a great honour that he should show an interest in you, and as he wishes to look at your eyes again you are to wait for him in the State Bed-Room tomorrow evening at nine o'clock."

"W-wait for the . . . Emperor?"

Vernita could hardly enunciate the words, she was so astonished.

"He will come by the garden door which leads into the Champs Élysées," the Princess said. "In that way no-one in the household except yourself will be aware that he is here."

"But why . . . why should he wish to . . . see me?" Vernita stammered.

Paulina smiled at the artlessness of the question.

"I imagine you have enough intelligence to know the answer to that," she replied.

"B-but . . . I cannot . . . I do not wish . . . to be alone with . . . the Emperor," Vernita stammered.

"Being a woman, you must realise that it is a great honour that the Emperor should even be aware of your existence."

The Princess turned round and saw the expression on Vernita's face.

"You must be pleasant and do whatever he wants. If not, there is certainly no place for you here in my household!"

She snapped out the last words, then went from from the bed-room, leaving Vernita staring after her with wide, frightened eyes.

Chapter Five

Vernita was feeling frantic.

The day had passed and there was no sign of the Count.

She felt that at any moment he would arrive at the Hôtel de Charost, but although during the morning she hung about at the top of the stairs hoping to see him in the Hall there was no sign of him.

Several other gentlemen called on the Princess while she was in the *Boudoir Violet,* choosing still more gowns and bonnets, but when she came upstairs to dress she spoke of spending the afternoon with a friend.

It was with difficulty that Vernita prevented herself from enquiring if the Count would go with her.

Instead she encouraged the Princess to talk, as she sometimes did when she was dressing, by asking artless questions about her party last night and the one she was to attend this evening.

The Princess could always be flattered into talking about herself, but though Vernita tried everything she could to inveigle her into mentioning the Count's name, she failed.

She realised that since the Emperor had noticed her the Princess was looking at her with interest and treating her as a human being.

The knowledge that the evening was approaching and she would either have to do as she was told

or else refuse a man who considered himself omnip-
otent filled Vernita with horror.

She was very innocent, but she knew that wom-
en like the Princess had lovers, and while she was
vague about what they did together she knew it was
something very intimate and very private.

The idea of any man except the Count touching
her made her feel sick and disgusted, and she knew
that she had felt violent revulsion against the Emperor yesterday when he had tried to kiss her.

She decided when she was alone during the afternoon that she would have to leave the Hôtel de
Charost, either of her own volition or because she
would be dismissed as the Princess had threatened.

She had not unpacked all the contents of her
trunk and now the few things she had removed because she wished to wear them she repacked and
was ready, she thought, to leave at a moment's notice.

At the same time, she knew she could not face
Paris alone unless she discussed the matter first with
the Count.

She supposed she could go back to her old room
in the Rue des Arbres. But she could not pay for it
unless she found work and the idea of walking the
streets looking for employment was too horrifying
to contemplate.

She tried to pray but she felt that it was impossible to do anything but cry out for her mother as a
child might have done.

"Help me, Mama, help me," she begged. "Tell me
what to do. Supposing he has left Paris ... and no
longer ... wants me?"

She could not believe that the love she felt for
the Count had been just a moment's rapture and
he had forgotten it already.

She had heard the sincerity in his voice when
he had said he loved her. She had seen the look in
his eyes and she did not credit that any man even if
he was the greatest actor in the world could have
been pretending so convincingly.

"I love him!" she whispered to herself.

She felt her whole body cry out to him, calling him because she was in danger, begging him to come to her side and help her.

Because she was so desperate, when it was now four o'clock in the afternoon and the Princess had returned and was lying down in her bed-room, Vernita went downstairs to ask the footmen in the Hall if they had seen the Count.

She pretended she had a message for him from the Princess but the flunkey shook his head.

"*Monsieur* has not been here today," he answered. "Perhaps he has found someone prettier to attract him, although that would be difficult."

He spoke with the familiarity of one servant to another, then as Vernita turned away in despair he said:

"Come out with me one evening. I'll give you a bit of fun."

"Thank you, but I have too much work to do," Vernita answered, and ran up the stairs thinking the footman would be surprised if he knew who else was calling tonight to see her.

She went to her room to sit down again, wondering what she should do, feeling that time was passing and that if the Count did not come she would have to make the decision herself—and before nine o'clock.

The door opened and one of the lady's-maids came in. She was carrying a dark blue velvet cloak over her arm and she held it out to Vernita.

"Be a Saint and mend this for me," she said. "I put it away thinking it'd not be needed again until the winter."

"Does Her Imperial Highness intend to wear it this evening?" Vernita asked.

The maid nodded.

"It's turned cold and as she's always half-naked she fancies she's already caught a chill."

There was no respect in the maid's voice and as she left the room she added:

"Hurry! She thinks I'm getting it out of the ward-

robe and she'll give me hell if she knows I put it
away without repairing it first."

Vernita knew this was true.

The Princess, for all her feckless ways, was extremely fussy about anything to do with her clothes
and indeed with the house.

She was indolent, but she always inspected the
household once a week, on Monday, insisting on
cleanliness in every department. Anything untidy so
infuriated her that she raged at the servants concerned until they trembled before her.

Taking on her lap the cloak which was lined
with satin and edged with snow-white ermine, Vernita quickly repaired the clasp which had come loose,
then ran down the back-stairs to the Princess's bed-
room.

She had nearly reached it when to her surprise
she saw a man pass through the door. She had only a
fleeting glimpse of him, but her heart gave a sudden
leap as she thought it must be the Count.

He was here—he was here at last! Now she
must find a moment in which to tell him what had
happened and ask him what she should do.

She went to the door and raised her hand to
knock and as she did so she heard the Princess ex-
claim:

"Napoleon! I was not expecting you at this hour!"

"I want to speak to you."

There was a pause while Vernita knew the two
lady's-maids withdrew into another room which com-
municated with the Princess's.

"What has happened? What is wrong?" Paulina
asked, and the Emperor replied:

"I came to see you immediately because I have
had a report from Fouché on this Swedish Count of
yours."

"From Fouché?" the Princess exclaimed angrily.
"You do not mean to say you have been having me
watched by that nasty, venomous rat? I hate him! He
spreads poison wherever he goes."

"I am aware of that," Napoleon replied, "but he also finds it in the most unlikely places."

There was a note in his voice that made his sister say after a moment:

"What are you trying to tell me?"

"Fouché thinks," the Emperor said slowly, "although he is not yet absolutely sure, that this man who calls himself Count Axel de Storvik is a spy in the pay of the English."

"I do not believe it!" Paulina answered. "How does he know? Why should he imagine such a thing?"

"The Swedish Ambassador vouched for his *bona fides*, but there is a clerk in the Swedish Embassy who tells a very different tale."

"A clerk?" Paulina said scornfully. "What should he know?"

The Emperor walked across the room and back again.

"Fouché has some hold over the man. Anyway, under Police interrogation he says that Couriers have been sent from Paris by the Count sometimes two or three times a week."

"Where to?" Paulina enquired.

"Ostensibly to Sweden," the Emperor replied, "but the informer thinks that that was merely a blind and the information they carried was intended for our enemies."

"If you ask me, the whole thing is a lot of moonshine!" Paulina retorted rudely. "I cannot imagine anyone less like a spy than Axel. He is also Swedish and you know as well as I do that that country is neutral."

"I am not so sure about that," the Emperor replied. "There have been rumours, admittedly very vague, that the Swedes have come to some arrangement with England."

"I do not believe it!" Paulina exclaimed again. "And if Axel is an enemy why should he be trying to sell you a gun which will undoubtedly use against the English? And perhaps against Sweden as well?"

"That is certainly a point in his favour," the Emperor admitted, "but quite frankly, Paulina, I do not like what I have heard!"

"I never like anything I hear from Fouché!" the Princess said petulantly.

"He is quite certain that this man is telling him the truth about the Couriers, and he is confident he will reveal more if he is paid or threatened sufficiently."

"I will not believe a word of what you have been telling me until I have positive proof of it," Paulina declared.

"We shall get that sometime this evening," the Emperor replied. "The Swedish clerk is with the Secret Police at the moment and Fouché has gone now to the Ministry to find out what they have learnt."

"Then we will wait until we are told."

"I shall take no action, of course, until I hear from Fouché again," the Emperor said. "But, my dear sister, on no account must you be seen with the Count this evening or at any other time."

"Why not?" the Princess asked crossly.

"That must be obvious," Napoleon replied. "You know as well as I do that if he is proved to be a spy, however much we may try to hush it up, all Paris will know about it and if his name is connected with yours there will undoubtedly be a scandal."

He sighed before he added:

"It is extraordinary, Paulina, how whatever you do seems to attract the very thing I am trying to avoid—gossip and speculation about the family."

"If you send Fouché ferreting down sewers you can hardly expect him to come up with anything except filth!"

"You do not appreciate the seriousness of this," Napoleon said sharply. "This man, De Storvik, has discussed military strategy with a number of my Generals. Even today I sent him myself to see General Berthier, who is at St. Cloud."

He made a sound of extreme irritation before he continued:

"Berthier, like Ney, is discreet, but God knows what Junot might have said to him before he left for Portugal."

"And you think any information he culled from them has been sent to Sweden?"

"I hope that is the only place to which it has gone."

"If you ask me, the whole intrigue exists only in the mind of Fouché," Paulina remarked. "You asked him to find out something unpleasant and he has found it. He would lose his reputation if he did anything else."

"We can only wait and see," Napoleon answered. "At the same time, this is an order, Paulina! You are not to see the man. You are not to communicate with him, and, above all, he is not to come to this house!"

Paulina gave a cry of sheer anger!

"I think you have made the whole thing up to deprive me of the one man I want to be with at this moment—the one man who amuses me."

"There are plenty of other men in Paris."

"But none as attractive as Axel!"

"If he is what we suspect he is," Napoleon said, "cannot you see, you stupid child, that he is merely using you as a means to meet the people from whom he can extract the information he needs?"

Paulina did not answer and after a moment he asked:

"Who introduced him to Junot?"

There was silence before reluctantly the Princess answered:

"I suppose I did. I cannot remember."

"I imagine Junot sent him to Ney and so on," the Emperor snapped. "The whole chain of events is obvious, and if you ask me for the truth I tell you that I consider it extremely likely that this man whom you think so attractive will end his life in front of a firing-squad!"

Paulina screamed.

"No, no! I will not have it!"

"There is nothing you can do to prevent it," Napoleon replied. "In the meantime, unless you want to be sent back to Rome with your husband, you will not communicate with this Swedish philanderer, nor will you mention his name in public."

"I hate you!" Paulina stormed. "I hate the way you always stop me from amusing myself and make me miserable!"

There was silence for a moment, then the Emperor said in a low voice that showed he was hurt:

"I am sorry, Paulina."

She did not reply and after a moment he said:

"I must go. I have to be at a Reception before the dinner, but I am returning here, as you know, later tonight, although I shall not see you."

"Why should you have your fun and I have none?" the Princess grumbled.

"Perhaps it will all prove to be a storm in a tea-cup," the Emperor replied, "but, to be honest I am not too hopeful."

Listening tensely outside the door, Vernita realised that the Emperor would now be leaving and hurriedly she turned and ran to hide herself on the back-stairs.

She heard the sound of the door opening then closing, and the Emperor passed the top of the stairs where she was hiding as he wended his way through a number of other rooms to reach the main staircase which led down to the Hall.

She knew that his Aides-de-Camp would be waiting for him and he would pass between lines of bowing footmen to his carriage that was in the courtyard.

She waited for a few minutes just to be certain he did not return, then she went to the Princess's door and knocked.

After a moment one of the lady's-maids opened it.

"I have brought the cloak for Her Imperial Highness."

"You can take it back," the maid answered. "It will not be needed this evening. Her Imperial Highness has decided to wear something different."

The maid shut the door without inviting Vernita in and she knew that now she was free—free to warn Axel and tell him he must leave Paris immediately.

She did not doubt for a moment that what Napoleon thought he had discovered was true.

Now she could understand why the Count had said that he might have to leave at a moment's notice Now she knew why he had said they must forget each other.

But more important even than that was the fact that he was not an enemy! He was not working, as she had thought, with the French against England.

It was wonderful news and she now loved him more than ever!

At the same time, Vernita knew he was in deadly danger and there was very little time for him to get away before Fouché's suspicions were confirmed.

She reached the ground floor and ran through various rooms towards the back of the house.

She entered the State Bed-Room, opened one of the long French windows, and stepped out into the garden.

Now she had only to speed through the shrubs and bushes to avoid being seen from the windows to reach the door in the wall which led into the Champs Élysées.

It was through this door, she remembered, that the Emperor intended to come in this evening when he expected her to be waiting for him in the State Bed-Room.

She let herself out cautiously, and now as she glanced up and down the road for fear that someone from the Hôtel de Charost should be watching, she realised it was beginning to rain and it was very cold.

It was only then that she was aware that she still held over her arm the blue velvet cloak that she had mended for the Princess.

Because she thought she would look less conspicuous wearing it than dressed only in the thin gown she had worn in the house, she swung it over her shoulders.

Pulling the hood over her head so that her face was framed with the white ermine, she started once again to run as quickly as she could to the Hôtel de Cleremont.

It was fortunate, she thought, that she had seen it before and knew where it was.

Standing back from the road, a courtyard in front of it with iron railings tipped with gold, it had, as she had said to the Count, a very impressive entrance.

But Vernita was at this moment concerned only with knocking as loudly as she could with the polished silver door-knocker.

The door was opened almost immediately and a flunkey wearing the claret-and-gold livery of the De Cleremonts waited for Vernita to speak.

"I wish to see Count Axel de Storvik."

"Is *Monsieur le Comte* expecting you, *Madame?*"

The flunkey was obviously impressed with the luxurious elegance of her fur-trimmed cloak and his question was respectful.

"Will you tell *Monsieur* that *Mademoiselle* Bernier wishes to see him immediately?"

Vernita had run so quickly through the garden and down the road that she sounded breathless.

As if the flunkey realised that her errand was urgent, he invited her in and showed her into a small Salon opening off the Hall.

It had an elegance that was very different from the flamboyant rooms of the Hôtel de Charost.

The furniture was covered in needle-point, the colours mellowed with age. The seventeenth- and eighteenth-century furniture was classically French and the pictures in the gilt frames were all of De Cleremont ancestors who had each contributed to the history of France.

But Vernita had no eyes for her surroundings. All she was thinking of was the Count and his safety.

Her heart was thumping violently in her breast and her fingers were trembling as she twisted them together, feeling frantically that time was passing and

Fouché and his Secret Police might be arriving at any moment.

The door opened and the Count stood there, an expression of surprise on his face.

"Vernita!" he exclaimed. "Why are you here? What has happened?"

She ran towards him to throw herself against him and as his arms went round her she said frantically:

"They have discovered that you are not what you appear to be. The Police may be coming to . . . arrest you at any moment. You must leave . . . Paris. You must get away . . . immediately!"

"What is all this? What are you saying to me?"

"I overheard the Emperor telling the Princess that he had instructed Chief of Police *Monsieur* Fouché to make enquiries about you. A clerk in the Swedish Embassy has told them of the many Couriers you sent to Sweden and he is also ready to reveal more of what he has seen and heard."

The Count's eyes were on Vernita's face as she spoke. Then he bent his head and kissed her forehead.

"Thank you, my darling!"

He took his arms from her and opened the door he had closed behind him on entering the room, and spoke to a flunkey outside.

"Send Henri to me immediately!"

"*Certainement, Monsieur le Comte.*"

The Count shut the door again.

"As you say I must leave Paris," he said, "I must also thank you for saving my life."

Vernita looked at him, then she said in a very low voice:

"P-please . . . take me with you."

"I cannot do that," the Count answered. "I may get away, but it would be desperately dangerous for you to be with me if I was arrested."

"You . . . do not understand. I . . . I am . . . English!"

"English?" the Count ejaculated.

"My parents and I were staying in Paris when the Armistice came to an end."

"And you might have been interned!" the Count exclaimed. "Why did I not think of it? Of course, that explains everything!"

"So . . . I may come with . . . you?" Vernita asked.

She thought he hesitated, and added:

"You must take me! The Emperor has commanded that I should . . . meet him . . . tonight in the room where you . . . found us yesterday."

"Curse him!" the Count said. "Yes, of course you must come with me!"

The door opened and a small man came into the room.

"You sent for me, *Monsieur?*"

"Yes, Henri, we have to leave at once! The hounds are on my heels!"

It seemed to Vernita that the man's expression did not change. He merely said:

"Everything is ready, *Monsieur.* I will take the cases down to the stables."

"Thank you, Henri."

The servant left the room and Vernita looked at the Count enquiringly.

"Henri and I were always expecting this might happen," he said. "But, my darling, you are quite sure that you are prepared to trust yourself to me?"

"I only know that I would rather . . . die with you than . . . live without you."

He held out his arms and once again Vernita threw herself into them. Now his lips found hers and he kissed her slowly, passionately, and possessively.

Then taking her by the hand he walked with her from the room and out into the Hall.

The Count spoke to the flunkey and he brought him a cape, his tall hat, and driving-gloves. Then once again taking Vernita's hand as if she were a child, he led her down a long passage until they emerged at the back of the house where the stables were situated.

Two ostlers were putting a pair of horses between the shafts of the chaise. Another was raising the hood. A footman was assisting Henri to strap the valises onto the back of the vehicle.

The Count handed Vernita into the chaise and placed a rug over her knees. Then he picked up the reins, Henri swung himself up into the seat at the back, and a few seconds later they were driving out of the courtyard and down a narrow street which led them back into the Champs Élysées.

It had all happened so quickly that Vernita felt as if she had hardly got her breath before they passed down a wide avenue which led them towards the Bois.

"Shall we get away?" she asked a little nervously.

They were the first words either of them had spoken since they had left the Hôtel de Cleremont.

"We will do our damnedest!" the Count answered.

Vernita gave a little cry of surprise.

"You can speak English!"

"It is not surprising," he answered, "as it happens to be my native language!"

She turned to stare at him in astonishment.

"You are English?"

"My real name is Tregarron," he answered, "Lord Tregarron. Let me explain that my disguise was somewhat easy because I have a Swedish grandmother and the Storviks are in fact my relatives."

"But the Emperor said the Swedish Ambassador had vouched for you."

"He thought I was my cousin who is also called Axel, and who is the real Count Axel de Storvik. He happens to be six years older than I am."

"It was very brave of you!" Vernita said, her eyes shining. "I never dreamt for one moment that you were English, otherwise of course I would have told you who I was."

"It was exceedingly obtuse of me not to realise what you were," Axel answered, "but you spoke such perfect French, and I have learnt in the game I play to be very suspicious of those who are not word-perfect in the part they play."

"I am glad you thought my French was good," Vernita said. "I was taught by an émigré family to whom Mama and Papa offered their hospitality during the Revolution. There were two children of about my own age, so French became as familiar to me as my own language."

"That accounts for it," Axel answered, "but I should have been suspicious when you told me that your horse was called Dragonfly."

Vernita gave a little laugh.

"I realised I had made a slip, but I spoke without thinking. Am I dreaming or is it really true that we are together and there are no more secrets between us?"

"It is true," Axel answered slowly. "But, my darling, if we are caught, you realise how terrible the consequences will be? I do not think they will shoot you, but you will certainly be imprisoned for the duration of the war."

"I am not afraid as long as I am with you," Vernita replied.

He turned to smile down at her. Then she said:

"Perhaps I should have asked sooner, but where are we going?"

"We are going South," Axel answered. "Henri and I always decided that if we had to escape it would be foolish to go North, which is what the Police, the military, or whoever else was after us, would consider likely, and we would therefore make for Marseilles."

"Can you trust Henri?" Vernita asked.

"With my life, as he trusts me with his!" Axel replied.

He concentrated on passing a number of vehicles, then he explained:

"Henri was groom to the *Duc* de Trevise, one of the most ancient families in France, but he killed a soldier who was trying to rape his sister. He escaped arrest and crossed in a smugglers' boat to England."

"That was clever of him," Vernita said, fascinated by the story.

"Unfortunately, the smugglers took from him every *sou* he had on him and he was brought to my notice when he was caught stealing turnips from a field on my estate because he had had nothing to eat for several days."

"And you gave him shelter?" Vernita asked.

"I took him into my employment," Axel replied. "It was during the Armistice, when I had left the Army in which I had fought for over five years. But I felt, as did a number of other people in England, that what we were experiencing was just the calm before another storm."

"Papa believed we should have peace at last," Vernita said wistfully.

"That is what everybody hoped," Axel replied, "but I knew how insatiably ambitious Napoleon was and that he would never rest until he had conquered the whole world."

"Do you think he will . . . succeed?" Vernita's voice was very low.

"Not while England exists! Of that I am completely and absolutely certain!"

"And when the war started again you became a spy?"

"That is rather an unpleasant word for it," Axel said with a twist of his lips, "but basically that is what happened."

"And you thought it would be easy to get information if you came to France under the identity of your cousin."

"It was a plan that was carefully thought out," Axel explained. "I discussed it with the Prime Minister and of course the Foreign Office and a number of Army Commanders who were very anxious to know what sort of weapons the French had."

"Then the Emperor was right," Vernita said with a little cry. "He said to the Princess that Marshal Ney and General Junot might have given you military information which would be valuable to the enemies of France."

"Napoleon was always extremely astute," Axel conceded. "That is exactly what they did. That was why I insisted on bringing with me from England a design for a gun that is far superior and more mobile than anything the French are using at the moment."

"Will they not make it themselves?" Vernita asked.

"They may try, but it would take time to develop. Meanwhile, our Army already has a small number of these guns and will have a great many more in the near future."

Vernita clapped her hands.

"That was clever! So very clever of you! And although you must now try to get away, what you have already learnt will help our country."

"I believe the information I have been able to send back is extremely valuable, as long as it gets there."

"Do you think it will?"

"I am sure of it. The Diplomatic Couriers carried my reports and Sweden is ostensibly neutral."

"The Emperor sounded rather doubtful about that."

"He is quite right to be. I will tell you something which I doubt will be able to be kept a secret for much longer."

"What is that?" Vernita asked.

"On December third, the day after Napoleon was crowned Emperor, we English signed a secret agreement with Sweden securing for the sum of eighty thousand pounds the Baltic island of Rügen and the fortress of Stralsund."

"Why should we want those places?" Vernita asked.

"For an Anglo-Russian landing on the Pomeranian mainland."

"And you think that will help to defeat Napoleon?"

"I think it will prove to be one more nail in his coffin," Axel replied.

As he finished speaking he sighed.

"We have a long way to go yet. For the moment Napoleon is the dominant power in the whole Continent and most other nations are far too frightened to oppose him in any way."

Vernita was silent, thinking how confident of himself the Emperor had seemed and how idolised he was by his countrymen, to whom he had brought glittering victories and a sense of power they had not known for generations.

She did not speak for a little while. Then Axel looking at her said:

"You are looking very rich and grand all of a sudden!"

"I am afraid I have . . . stolen this cloak."

"It certainly becomes you."

She blushed at the expression in his eyes. Then as he attended to his horses again she said:

"You realise I have nothing with me except for what I stand up in?"

"We will buy what you need," Axel answered.

"You must be careful not to spend your money too quickly," Vernita cautioned, remembering how her father's money had gradually disappeared and she and her mother had grown poorer and poorer.

As if Axel thought the same thing he said:

"Do not worry. Tonight I intend staying with a friend of mine who will lend me all the money I need until we can find a ship to carry us home."

"A friend?" Vernita asked.

"The *Vicomte* de Cleremont, with whom I have been staying in Paris. He is at the moment at one of his country estates near Merlun, which is where we are going at this moment."

"He will be brave enough to hide us even if he knows the Secret Police are looking for you?"

"You will like my friend," Axel said. "He belongs to one of the aristocratic families of France who loathe and detest Napoleon, whom they consider to be an upstart—and a Corsican, not a Frenchman!"

Vernita laughed.

"That is exactly what the servants said when they were talking frankly about their mistress."

"The old *Régime* are very proud and the *Vicomte* de Cleremont is one of my closest friends. We were at University together and he has often stayed with me in England."

"So you trusted him when you came to France."

"Like Henri I was quite happy to put my life in his hands."

"It frightens me when you say that," Vernita said.

"I am so fortunate to have so many people who care for me," Axel smiled, "and especially you, my precious."

"I have been so worried and unhappy all day," Vernita told him. "When the Princess told me last night that the Emperor wanted me to meet him at nine o'clock in the State Bed-Room, I was so frightened I could only think that I must tell you and ask you what I should do."

"I could not come to the Hôtel de Charost today," Axel replied.

"I know that now. I heard the Emperor tell the Princess that he had sent you to St. Cloud to see General Berthier."

"When I received the message, there was no way of telling you that I was leaving Paris very early," Axel explained, "but I knew the Princess was dining out and I intended to wait until she had left the house and then ask to see you."

"The servants would have been very surprised!"

"I would have found some excuse," Axel said lightly. "All that mattered was that you should not be worried or upset."

He paused before he added:

"I knew what you must have felt when I came into the State Bed-Room yesterday and saw you in the arms of the Emperor."

"Were you...angry?" Vernita asked in a low voice.

"I knew that it was not your fault," Axel replied, "but if any Emperor ever risked being knocked down, Napoleon missed that indignity by a hair's-breath."

"You could not have done that!" Vernita exclaimed. "Heaven knows what would have happened to you!"

"That did pass through my mind," Axel replied, "but I thought, my dearest one, I was more useful to you alive than dead or at best locked up in the Bastille."

"I was so surprised. I had been sent down to find one of the Princess's ear-rings which she had left on the ... bed-side table...."

As she spoke she remembered what she had thought, and her suspicion of the reason for the Princess Paulina having left one of her ear-rings behind.

The colour rose in her face, and she stared blindly ahead, aware of nothing but the jealousy within her breast.

Axel transferred the reins into his right hand and reaching out his left took Vernita's hand in his and raised it to his lips.

She had no gloves and his lips were hard and possessive against the softness of her skin.

"I love you!" he said in his deep voice. "Forget the past, forget everything except that we are together as we want to be and as fate intended."

Vernita felt herself vibrate to his words, the tone in which he said them, and the touch of his lips.

She moved a little nearer to him and looked up, her eyes shining as she whispered:

"I love you ...I love you so much that nothing ...nothing in the world ...matters but you."

"That is what I want you to say," Axel replied, "and also what I want you to think."

He released her hand, then he said in a different tone of voice:

"We both have to think very seriously and carefully as we plan for the future. From now on any slip of the tongue or any unwary action will result in our losing our happiness and each other."

"I know that," Vernita said. "Oh, Axel, Axel, help me to be as clever as you, to play a . . . part so that no-one will . . . suspect."

Axel smiled, then he said:

"I have the feeling, Vernita, that we shall succeed in what we are attempting because we are so close to each other and because we have everything to gain—and equally everything to lose."

Vernita put her hand on his arm.

"You are right," she said in a low voice. "We shall win because I know that Papa and Mama will be helping us, and because I shall be praying every moment of the day and night that we shall reach England together in safety."

"England and home!" Axel said softly.

His eyes met hers and Vernita knew that was what they both wanted—to be home and together for the rest of their lives.

Chapter Six

They had driven for some way and were well outside the suburbs of Paris in the tree-covered countryside.

Vernita had found it impossible not to keep looking back over her shoulder to see if they were being followed by soldiers or mounted Police.

Although Axel had assured her that Minister Fouché and doubtless the Emperor would assume they had gone Northwards, she could not help feeling afraid.

Axel's horses were moving at a sharp pace and she tried to convince herself that there was no reason to be fearful for the moment unless Fouché was more perceptive than they imagined.

Vernita had not spoken for some time, but now she asked:

"You do not think your friend will be afraid to shelter you when he learns of the Emperor's suspicions?"

Axel smiled.

"I will let you into a secret by telling you that Etienne de Cleremont has sheltered a great many refugees in the last two years and is in fact an avowed enemy of the present *Régime*."

"Surely that is very dangerous?"

Axel shrugged his shoulders before he said:

"At the moment Napoleon is wooing the real French aristocracy and seeking their support. He knows that in the Courts of Europe he is regarded as an upstart. In fact, the Emperor of Austria, who is the head of Europe's oldest Royal Line, has rejected all his overtures of friendship."

"It is very brave of your friend the *Vicomte* to help those who are trying to escape from France," Vernita said. "I wish we had known about him when ... Mama was ... alive."

"I wish so too," Axel replied, "but what is important, my darling, is that you should be safe."

"And you," Vernita said in a soft voice.

He looked at her for a moment with a smile on his lips and the expression in his eyes made her heart leap.

Then he was urging on the horses as if it was more important than anything else to arrive quickly at the *Vicomte*'s house, where they would be safe.

At the same time, when finally they reached the outskirts of Fontainebleau, having stopped only once to eat a light repast at a small isolated Inn, Vernita felt apprehensive.

It was one thing, she thought, for the *Vicomte* to be prepared to look after his friend and keep him safe, but she was well aware that in a situation like this, women were a nuisance and she had the feeling that she was positively an encumbrance.

It was very late in the afternoon when finally they drove up a drive bordered with lime trees to where in the distance there was a *Château*, grey with wooden shutters.

"This is only one of my friend's country estates," Axel said as he drove the horses round the gravel sweep towards the front door, "and fortunately one which is less well-known. If Fouché searches for me, he is more likely to go to the Castle in the Loire Valley, which is the ancestral home of the De Cleremonts."

He drew his horses to a standstill and grooms came running from the stables. Then before they had stepped out of the chaise the front door was opened and there were servants to welcome them.

"*Bonjour,* Jacques!" Axel said to an elderly man. "Is *Monsieur le Vicomte* at home?"

"*Oui, Monsieur le Comte,*" the servant replied, "if you and *Madame* will follow me."

He led them across an attractive Hall and opened the door of a Salon whose windows over-looked a large garden.

A lady and gentleman were sitting together on a sofa and as the servant announced "*Monsieur le Comte* Axel de Storvik" they both sprang to their feet.

"Axel!" the *Vicomte* exclaimed. "What brings you here? What has happened?"

"You know the answer to that."

Axel walked across the room and taking the out-stretched hand of the lady raised it to his lips.

"It is delightful to see you, Marie-Claire," he said, "even if it is in somewhat unfortunate circumstances."

Two dark eyes looked up into his apprehensively.

"They have discovered who you are?" she asked.

"It is not quite as bad as that," Axel replied. "But they are suspicious of my credentials."

As he spoke he turned to Vernita, who was standing a little behind him, and drew her forward.

"May I introduce Miss Vernita Waltham?" he asked. "She has been hiding for two years in a Paris attic, frightened that she and her family might be interned."

The *Vicomtesse* gave a little cry and put out both her hands to Vernita.

"You poor child!" she said. "It must have been terrible! But Axel found you."

"We found each other," he replied, "and now you see I have a two-fold motive to escape Fouché's blood-hounds."

"Will he suspect that you would come here?" the *Vicomte* enquired.

"I hope not," Axel replied. "I left the letter for them to find telling you that I had to leave for Sweden on urgent business."

"I wondered when we would have to use that," the Vicomte remarked.

"And Henri told the ostlers that we were travelling North."

"Well, that should put Fouché off your tracks for the moment, at any rate," the *Vicomte* remarked, "but one can never be certain."

"I am sure Miss Waltham would like to come upstairs and wash," the *Vicomtesse* said. "When did you last have anything to eat?"

"It seems a long time ago," Axel admitted. "And it was not a very substantial meal, as we were in a hurry."

"Then you need a large dinner." The *Vicomtesse* smiled.

"There is one thing I want to ask you," Axel said, looking at his friend the *Vicomte*.

"What is that?"

"Would it be possible to arrange for Vernita and me to be married?"

If Axel surprised his friend, Vernita was astonished.

Then as he looked at her and as her eyes met his, she knew it was what they both wanted and because they loved each other it was inevitable.

"Married?" the *Vicomte* exclaimed. "But of course it would be possible! Dear old Father Gérard, although he has retired, is still living in the village. We can trust him with our innermost secrets and he would never betray us. I will send for him at once."

Vernita felt it was perhaps typical of the *Vicomte* that he made no comment: he merely accepted the situation and was prepared to do exactly what his friend wished.

"We would not . . . want you to take any . . . risks on our behalf," Vernita said in a hesitating voice.

At the same time, she could not help putting out her hand and slipping it into Axel's.

His fingers closed over hers and she felt him protecting her and knew that the only thing that mat-

tered was that she should belong to him. If they were
to be taken prisoner they would be taken together.

"Everything shall be arranged, Axel," the *Vicomte* promised, "but the ceremony must be late at
night after the servants have gone to bed. We can
trust them, as you know; at the same time, the less
they know, the better."

"Of course," Axel agreed.

The *Vicomtesse* linked her arm through Vernita's
and drew her towards the door.

"This is very exciting!" she said. "We must make
you look beautiful for Axel, who is one of our dearest
and most loved friends."

"I am afraid I have nothing... nothing except the
clothes I am ... wearing," Vernita replied. "You see,
when I overheard what the Emperor was saying to the
Princess Paulina, I ran straight to your house in the
Champs Élysées, where I knew Axel was staying."

"You overheard the Emperor?" the *Vicomtesse*
exclaimed. "You were in the Hôtel de Charost? Tell me
everything! Tell me from the very beginning."

As they walked up the stairs Vernita began the
story and soon they reached a very attractive bed-
room on the first floor with a bed draped in white
muslin.

It was as fresh and charming as the spring flowers outside in the garden.

She gave a little cry of pleasure and exclaimed:

"What a lovely room! And how pretty your house
is!"

"I expect you would find any place pretty after
living in an attic for so long," the *Vicomtesse* said
sympathetically. "Now we have to think of something
pretty for you to wear for your wedding. Your cloak is
certainly resplendent!"

"It is not mine! It belongs to the Princess Paulina," Vernita replied. "I had forgotten that I had it
over my arm until I reached the Champs Élysées,
and then because it was raining I put it on."

"It is certainly very becoming," the *Vicomtesse*

said, "but you must be married in white, and fortunately I have just remembered that I have the De Cleremont family veil here because my sister borrowed it last month and I have not yet returned it to the Castle."

"A veil!" Vernita exclaimed, and her eyes were shining.

She knew that she wanted to look beautiful for Axel. He had seen her only in the common black dress she had borrowed from Louise and the mauve gown in which she had dined with him and which had really been her mother's.

There was not a woman in the world, she thought, who would not wish to wear white on her wedding-day.

Although she tried to protest to the *Vicomtesse* that she must not be any trouble, she knew it was very half-hearted because the only thing that really mattered was that she should look the sort of bride that Axel wanted.

The *Vicomtesse* ordered a bath for Vernita, and whilst she was bathing she felt that the warm water not only washed away the dust of the journey but also much of the tenseness which she had felt ever since they drove away from Paris.

When she had dried herself and was putting on her chemise, the *Vicomtesse* came into the bed-room carrying a white evening-gown. It looked very fragile and was decorated with frills of net at the hem and the *décolletage*.

"It is very simple," the *Vicomtesse* said, "but I think it will suit you."

"It is lovely!" Vernita exclaimed.

Everything she had herself was two years old and, although perhaps only a woman would have noticed the difference, the line had altered and gowns were more elaborate than they had been in 1803.

She put it on and the *Vicomtesse* exclaimed with delight.

"It is only too large in the waist," she said, "but then you are so thin."

As she spoke she looked at Vernita and added softly:

"I know why, and I am sorry. It must have been terrible for you, knowing you could not buy the things your mother needed."

"I only wish Mama could be here today," Vernita answered. "She would have been so glad that I have found somebody like Axel."

"I think any mother would be pleased to know her daughter was marrying such a marvellous person," the *Vicomtesse* replied. "My husband has known Axel far longer than I have, but we both think he is an exceptional person with very fine character."

"And very brave," Vernita added.

"That goes without saying," the *Vicomtesse* agreed, "but though a man's courage makes one proud, it also gives one heart-ache."

She spoke with a little throb in her voice which told Vernita that she was often afraid for her husband.

"Are we being very selfish in inflicting ourselves upon you when it might cause you a great deal of trouble?" Vernita asked.

The *Vicomtesse* smiled.

"Do you think Etienne thinks it a trouble? He has helped so many people. Yet, although I would not have him otherwise, it always makes me afraid that one day he will go too far and end up either in prison or on the guillotine!"

"I feel ashamed that we should ask so much," Vernita said humbly.

The *Vicomtesse* made a little gesture with her hand.

"What are friends for?" she asked. "We want to help you. We are ashamed that France should have caused so much suffering and so many unnecessary deaths all over Europe."

She gave a deep sigh that seemed to come from the very depths of her being before she said:

"Perhaps one day there will be peace—but not, I am convinced, while Napoleon is alive."

Then with a quick change of mood she said:

"But do not let us talk of anything that is un-happy or dismal on your wedding-day."

"A very surprising wedding-day!" Vernita smiled. "We had not even spoken of getting married until now."

"But you knew you were meant for each other," the *Vicomtesse* said softly.

"I think we knew it as soon as we met," Vernita answered simply.

The *Vicomtesse* called a maid and told her to take in the white gown round the waist so that it would fit tightly and reveal Vernita's exquisite fig-ure.

They did not speak in front of the servant of the marriage that was to take place, and only when Vernita was ready and they went downstairs to-gether did the *Vicomtesse* say:

"We will come up after dinner to put on your veil, and I have a diamond tiara with which to hold it in place."

"You are so kind," Vernita said.

The maid had arranged her hair in a fashionable style and she felt as she went downstairs that Axel would not be ashamed of her in front of his friends.

The *Vicomtesse* was not beautiful, but she had a very sweet face with dark, expressive eyes and jet-black hair which glowed with blue lights.

She was beautifully dressed and walked with a grace which somehow echoed the pride and distinc-tion which was very apparent in her husband.

The two gentlemen were waiting for them in the Salon, and as Vernita entered the room she thought it would be impossible to find anywhere in the world two men who looked so distinguished and had such authority in their bearing.

As she walked towards Axel, Vernita was watch-ing the expression on his face to see if he was pleased with her appearance. No woman could have mistaken the gleam in his eyes and the smile on his lips for anything but admiration.

As she reached him he put out his hand and took
hers.

"I hope you approve of your future wife's appearance," the *Vicomtesse* said. "Later she will look
even more like a bride. That is, if Etienne has everything arranged."

"Father Gérard will arrive at nine-thirty," the *Vicomte* said. "I have ordered a carriage to collect him."

Vernita felt Axel's fingers press hers and she
knew he was telling her without words that he was
impatient to make her his wife.

She felt herself thrill at the thought. Then the
Vicomte poured out some champagne and he and
his wife raised their glasses.

"To the Bride and Groom!"

Axel smiled and Vernita blushed. Then the
Vicomte said:

"I always warned you that one day you would
fall in love, Axel, but you were so positive that you
preferred to remain a bachelor."

"It was what I thought was essential in the life
I was living," Axel answered, "but when I met Vernita I knew my wandering days were over."

The *Vicomte* looked surprised.

"Do you mean that?"

"If by the grace of God we get home safely,"
Axel answered, "I intend to settle down on my estates
and play my part when necessary in the House of
Lords."

Vernita's fingers tightened on his.

"I am glad, so very glad," she said. "I do not think
I could ... bear to be left behind ... thinking of you
in danger ... wondering if you would return to me."

"That is how I knew you would feel," Axel said in
his deep voice. Then he added with a twinkle in his
eye: "But then I suppose everyone must make sacri-
fices when they marry, and mine must be to give up
trying to put my head in a noose, or should I say under a guillotine?"

The *Vicomtesse* gave a little cry of horror.

"You are not to say such things!"

"Forgive me, Marie-Claire," Axel pleaded. "I should not make your 'flesh creep,' as my old Nurse used to say."

The *Vicomte* laughed.

"Mine said exactly the same thing, but with reason—for we were all involved in the Revolution."

"That reminds me," the *Vicomtesse* said. "You will find our Chapel is still in a very bad state. It was badly damaged during the Revolution and although we have repaired the house itself, you know that it was only three years ago, in 1802, that Napoleon allowed the Churches to be opened again. So we have not had time to do much to the Chapel."

"It was thinking of the closed Churches and the scarcity of Priests, which made me wonder if it would be possible for you to arrange our marriage," Axel said.

"You were quite right to think that it might be a problem," the *Vicomte* replied. "When Napoleon reopened the Churches he was faced with finding sixty Bishops!"

"And some of them are terrible!" the *Vicomtesse* added.

"Well, at least people can go to Church if they wish to do so," Axel said.

"That is true," the *Vicomtesse* agreed. "Do you know, one old woman in the village said with gratitude: 'The Emperor must be a good man because he has given us back our Sunday.'"

They went in to dinner and now because the servants were present the *Vicomte* and Axel joked with each other and reminisced about their boyhood until the *Vicomtesse* and Vernita laughed with tears in their eyes.

Only when dinner was finished and they all walked towards the Salon did the *Vicomtesse* draw Vernita up the stairs to her bed-room.

"The servants have their meal after us," she said, "so there will be no maids about to see me arrange your veil, and only old Jacques will be on duty, who has looked after my husband since he was a boy and knows all our secrets."

She made Vernita sit down on the stool in front of the dressing-table and brought from a box an exquisite Brussels-lace veil which was so fine that it might have been made by a fairy's fingers.

She arranged it on Vernita's head, covering her face, and to hold it in place she put the diamond tiara on her head.

It was a very beautiful one, fashioned like a wreath of flowers, and each leaf was flexible so that when Vernita moved it glittered almost as if the flowers themselves were alive.

"You look very lovely!" the *Vicomtesse* said. "And now, as I heard Father Gérard arrive a few minutes ago, I think we should go downstairs."

Vernita was feeling shy and because the veil covered her face she felt as if she were isolated in a world by herself.

Quite suddenly it swept over her how strange this all was. She was marrying a man she had first seen only a few days ago, a man of whom she knew very little except that her heart trusted him and her soul told her that he was her fate.

It all seemed unbelievable when she thought of the two years she had spent in the attic speaking to nobody but her mother, the Danjous, and a few shop-keepers.

Then quite suddenly, almost as if the sun had come out in the darkness, her whole life was changed.

She knew that even if she had only a short time to live as Axel's wife, she would always be deeply and humbly grateful that God had been so kind to her.

As she and the *Vicomtesse* went downstairs she saw that the *Vicomte* was waiting for her in the Hall.

He was holding in his hand a small bouquet of white flowers, which he handed to her, offering her his arm at the same time.

The *Vicomtesse* disappeared and Vernita knew she had gone ahead to the Chapel.

Then the *Vicomte* led her down a long passage until they came to the Chapel, which was grey and old and, as they had said, in a bad state of repair.

Many of the glass windows were boarded up and the heads had been knocked off the statues of the Saints.

But there were six candles on the altar and flowers arranged on either side of it.

The Chapel seemed very quiet and empty as Vernita, on the *Vicomte*'s arm, walked up the aisle to where Axel was waiting.

She had the feeling as she neared him that they were meeting across eternity.

Nothing and nobody could ever stop them from belonging to each other because they were in reality one person who, having been divided, now through the mercy of God had come together again.

As she reached Axel she looked up at him and saw an expression on his face that told her all she wanted to know.

The cynicism and even the hard look of authority had gone and he was a man in love, a man who had found everything for which he had searched for a long time.

The Priest was very old, but he pronounced the beautiful words of the Service with a sincerity which came from his heart and he said them without the need of a prayer-book.

Vernita was not a Catholic, but she and her mother had attended a Catholic Church every Sunday in Paris because the Danjous would have thought it strange if they had not done so.

She had learnt to understand the Latin services and enjoy them.

"God hears our prayers," she told herself, "and whatever the religion may be to which a Church is dedicated, it is still the House of God."

Now she thought nothing could be more moving

or more sacred than the vows she and Axel were making to each other.

When finally they knelt to receive the blessing, Vernita knew that they were truly blessed and she felt in that moment that she was not alone in the Chapel with her husband.

Her mother and father were there too, and those who had loved him when he was a child, and perhaps many of their ancestors who had passed to another world yet were still to be a part of the love they were feeling.

When they rose from their knees, Axel lifted Vernita's veil from her face and bent to kiss her.

It was a kiss without passion, a kiss of dedication, and she knew that in it he repeated the vows he had just made, confirming that they were united and belonged to each other for all time.

Holding Axel's arm, she walked beside him from the Chapel back along the passage into the Hall.

She expected him to take her into the Salon, but instead, to her surprise, he started to climb the stairs.

She looked at him as if for explanation and he said quietly:

"I do not think that either of us wants to talk to anyone else and I hope you want to be alone with me, my darling, as I want to be alone with you."

There was a note in his voice which made Vernita feel as if he spoke in music. Then he took her not into the room which she had used before dinner but into another, farther down the passage, which was larger and more impressive.

It was a very beautiful room with a State Bed draped with blue curtains falling from a gold corola, but as Axel shut the door Vernita had eyes only for him.

He came to her side and stood looking down at her.

"You are everything I ever dreamt my wife should be," he said, "and it is hard for me to tell you in words how much I love you."

"Is it really . . . true that we are . . . married?" Vernita asked.

"We are married," he answered, "but if you wish, my darling, when we reach England we will be married again, because I know you are not a Catholic."

"It would be impossible to have a more beautiful wedding," Vernita replied, "but is it legal?"

"According to the laws of France we should also go in front of the Mayor," Axel replied, "but in every other country of the world the ceremony in which we have just taken part is valid, so you are indeed my wife."

"That is all I . . . want to be."

"Are you sure?" he asked.

"Very . . . very sure," she replied, lifting her face to his.

He did not kiss her; instead, he took the tiara from her head and lifted the veil from her hair.

Then he put his arms round her and pulled her against him as if he could no longer control his need for her.

"I love you, Vernita!" he said. "I love you beyond words, almost beyond thought. You are mine as I knew you must be when you looked at me with an expression of helplessness in your eyes."

As he spoke his lips came down on hers and he kissed her as he had before, so that she felt the rapture and wonder of it move up through her body like a shaft of sunlight.

Now the sensations he aroused in her were more wonderful, more exciting, even than they had been before, and she pressed herself closer against him while he kissed her demandingly, passionately, not only on her lips but on her eyes, her cheeks, and the softness of her neck.

"I want you, God knows I want you!" he said hoarsely, "but, my darling, I will be very gentle because I have no wish to frighten you."

"I am not . . . frightened," Vernita whispered, "it is all so . . . perfect . . . so beautiful . . . just as I knew love would be, and you are the ... husband who was always the ... hero in my dreams."

"Is that true?" Axel asked.

"Yes ... except that you are more ... wonderful ... more magnificent than ... any man I could imagine," Vernita replied.

He gave a laugh of sheer happiness, then he was kissing her again, kissing her wildly and frantically until she put her arms round his neck, wanting him closer and even closer.

He raised his head and looked down at her, at her flushed cheeks and her parted lips, at her eyes shining with emotions she did not understand.

She only knew that thrills swept through her body, making her feel as if she had come alive in a very different way from anything she had ever known before.

"You are so beautiful, so exquisite, that you are like a flower," Axel said passionately.

Vernita raised her lips to his, wanting him to kiss her again.

"My wife," he said softly, "my own precious wife, my love, my only love!"

She felt his hands undoing her white gown but his lips on hers made it impossible to think anymore.

* * *

The sun had barely risen before Vernita found herself driving away from the *Château*, having bade affectionate farewells to the *Vicomte* and *Vicomtesse*.

Axel had awoken her with a kiss so early that it was still dark. She had made a little murmur of happiness and tried to cuddle closer to him.

"We have to get up, my darling," he said.

"I ... love you," she whispered.

"And I love you," he answered, "more than I can ever begin to tell you!"

She put out her arm to pull his head down to hers, but he said:

"Wake up, my precious."

"I want you to kiss me," she murmured.

"I want not only to kiss you but to stay here all day making love to you," he answered. "But, my sweetheart, it is essential that we get to Marseilles as quickly as possible, unless we are to risk being captured."

His words were like a splash of cold water and Vernita sat up in bed; then, realising she was naked, she pulled the sheet against her bare breasts.

Axel laughed quietly and kissed her shoulder. Then he rose and went to the next room, where he knew Henri would already be waiting for him.

When she was alone Vernita got up quickly and started to wash.

She was just beginning to dress herself when the door opened and the *Vicomtesse* came in.

"I have brought you some clothes to wear," she said, "and I have also packed two valises with everything I think you will require for your journey to England. I hope I have forgotten nothing."

"I cannot take so much from you!" Vernita exclaimed.

"May I say it is a pleasure to give you anything," the *Vicomtesse* replied, "but Axel has said you are not to take your cloak with you because it would be too conspicuous, so I am compensated by knowing I shall have a most attractive new ermine hat and muff."

Vernita smiled.

"I was afraid I should not be able to own anything so magnificent for long!"

"I hope you will find the things I have packed for you are nearly as attractive," the *Vicomtesse* said, "and actually I have here a black velvet cloak trimmed with sable."

"But I cannot take anything so magnificent!" Vernita exclaimed. "And that gown is very lovely."

"I naturally wish you to look your best," the *Vicomtesse* said, "as you are impersonating me!"

"Impersonating you?" Vernita repeated in astonishment.

The *Vicomtesse* smiled.

"Axel is supposed to tell you what he and my husband planned, but I dare say you had other things to talk about last night!"

Vernita blushed and the *Vicomtesse* continued:

"Fouché's Police will be looking for a chaise containing Axel and an attractive girl wearing a blue velvet and ermine cape, so you must change your identity."

She smiled as she continued:

"We have disguised people in dozens of different ways; sometimes men have even been dressed as women so that they could get to the Swiss border. But Etienne thinks it would be far easier for people to accept you and Axel if they believe you to be *Vicomte* and *Vicomtesse* de Cleremont."

"Supposing ... the Police find you ... here?" Vernita asked.

"They will not," the *Vicomtesse* replied. "If anyone calls to enquire, they will be told that we have left for Nice, which is quite a reasonable place for us to be at this time of the year."

"Where will you really be?"

"We have a little Hunting-Lodge where we have sometimes hidden refugees. It is in the forest about fifteen miles from here. As far as we are aware, nobody knows of its existence except ourselves and two or three of our faithful servants. We will go there until we are sure that you have reached Marseilles and perhaps are on your way to England."

"It is so kind ... so very kind of you," Vernita exclaimed.

The *Vicomtesse* gave her a mischievous little smile.

"Shall I confess that to have Etienne alone with me and unconcerned with all the people he is helping will be like a second honeymoon?" she asked. "While you are enjoying yours, even though it may be a very unusual one, I shall be enjoying mine!"

Vernita bent forward and kissed her.

"How can I ever thank you?"

"By hurrying!" the *Vicomtesse* replied. "Other-

wise Axel will be annoyed with you, and Etienne
with me."

Her words galvanised Vernita into action and
quickly she put on the very attractive gown that
the *Vicomtesse* had brought her which had a smart
little jacket of the same material.

It was of dark green and very becoming, and
there was a bonnet, tied with the same ribbons and
decorated with silk flowers, which made her look
very elegant and at the same time very lovely.

"You may not need the cloak at the moment,"
the *Vicomtesse* said, "but when you get to sea it
might be cold, and it will certainly be rough and
windy in the Bay of Biscay."

Vernita drew in her breath.

It seemed as if they had such a very long way to
go before they reached England.

As if she knew what Vernita was thinking, the
Vicomtesse said:

"Do not worry. Etienne says I am clairvoyant
and I am utterly convinced that you will both reach
home in safety."

"I hope that this horrible war will be over soon
and you will be able to come and stay with us,"
Vernita said.

She gave a little laugh.

"It seems incredible, but I have never asked
Axel about his home. I have no idea what it is like or
even where it is!"

"You will find out," the *Vicomtesse* prophesied.
"It is very magnificent and exceedingly comfortable."

She provided Vernita also with a hand-bag in
which she was to find later some powder, lip-salve,
and a little enamel box which contained rouge—
something she had never previously used.

But now there was no time to do anything but
pick up her bag while the *Vicomtesse* carried her
cloak and they hurried downstairs to where break-
fast was waiting.

The *Vicomte* and Axel had already finished and

Vernita ate quickly and drank a cup of coffee, then went into the Hall.

Outside the open door she saw a smart Phaeton emblazoned with the coat of arms of the De Cleremonts.

There were four horses drawing it and two out-riders to accompany them on their journey.

"They will bring back the Phaeton when you reach Marseilles," the *Vicomte* said, as if Vernita had asked the question. "You can trust them. They are two men who have been with me for many years and they think it a great joke as well as an achievement that they can hood-wink Napoleon's troops or officials."

Then they were saying good-bye and driving off at such a fast pace that Vernita felt almost as if they flew through the air.

Only when they were on the main road which led towards Montargis did she say:

"I can hardly believe that two people could be so kind or do so much for their friend."

"I knew you would like Etienne and Marie-Claire," Axel said. "They are both very exceptional people and they loved you. They thought you were just the right sort of wife for me."

Vernita moved a little nearer to him before she asked:

"Is that what you . . . think too?"

"Can you doubt it?" he enquired. "When we are alone, close to each other as we were last night, I will tell you again that you are exactly the sort of wife I always wanted, and mean to keep."

Regardless of the fact that Henri was sitting behind them and the hood was down, Vernita put her cheek for a moment against his arm.

"I love you!" she said in a voice that only he could hear.

"If you talk like that," he said, "I shall kiss you and we shall be in imminent danger of having an accident!"

"Then I will be good," she said. "Oh, Axel, last night was so wonderful, so perfect, that I want to go down on my knees at every Church we come to and thank God that I am your wife."

"I feel the same," he answered. "Did I make you happy?"

"More happy than I can ever tell you," she answered, "and after these last two years when I thought I should never find anyone to love, it is as if a miracle has happened. In fact that is what it is!"

Axel's eyes were on his horses and she added after a moment with a little sigh:

"Louise was always saying to me, '*vous coifferez Saint Catherine,*' but now, incredibly and wonderfully, I am a married woman!"

"I am afraid I even had to borrow your wedding-ring," Axel said.

"I wondered where you could have got one, but I supposed the *Vicomte* had lent it to you."

"It belonged to his mother and I promised that when I buy you one in England I would keep this until he can come and collect it."

Vernita put her right hand over her left so that she could feel the ring under her glove.

"The eternal circle," she murmured. "It symbolises that our marriage shall be unbroken and we shall be together for eternity."

"Can you imagine for a moment that I would ever let you go?" Axel asked.

There was a note in his voice which made Vernita thrill.

Then because she felt an irrepressible yearning to be in his arms, she forced herself to think of other things.

"How long will it take us to reach Marseilles?" she asked.

"I was talking about that with Etienne," the Count replied, "and he tells me that a *diligence*, which is the same as our stage-coaches, travels every other day from Paris to Lyons and takes six days for the journey. They of course stop far more often than we will, so I reckon that with these horses, even though we have to give them plenty of rest, we should reach Lyons in four and a half days."

"And to Marseilles?" Vernita enquired.

"Three days more."

Vernita did not answer and after a moment Axel said:

"I am afraid you will find the Inns very uncomfortable, my darling, but we have brought our own bed-linen with us as well as blankets."

Vernita looked at him in surprise and he explained:

"It is the way the *Vicomte* de Cleremont and his wife would always travel, and you will be glad to hear I have plenty of money to buy the best accommodation possible. But Etienne told me to warn you that the best is not very good."

"Nothing matters as long as we are together," Vernita said.

"That is what I thought," Axel agreed. "What we must be careful of is to avoid meeting anyone who actually knows Etienne and Marie-Claire."

He paused and went on after a moment:

"It is unlikely, but as an 'old hand' at this sort of game I know we have to take every precaution."

"What must we do?" Vernita asked.

"Be seen in public as little as possible, and when we arrive at an Inn, Henri will arrange everything before we get there."

"How will he do that?"

"He will ride the horse of one of the out-riders, who will take his place on the Phaeton. We will wait outside the town or village, then drive up with a flourish of trumpets, so to speak, hoping they are impressed with our importance."

He laughed before he continued:

"As soon as we get to the door, Henri will help you alight and you will hurry into the Inn and up the stairs holding a handkerchief up to your face as if you feel faint or carriage-sick. I will follow you as quickly as possible. We will dine alone in a private

Sitting-Room or, if we cannot obtain one, in our bed-room."

"I should like that," Vernita said impulsively.

"So shall I," Axel replied in his deep voice.

He glanced at her and added:

"It will be a strange honeymoon, my darling, and a rather nerve-racking one. At the same time, definitely it is our honeymoon and I dare say there will be compensations!"

"If you mean by that that I shall be happy," Vernita said, "I only want to tell you that I love you and keep on saying it."

"And I love you, my precious darling."

She looked up at him with a smile and he bent his head for a fraction of a second and kissed her on the lips.

Then as she thrilled at his touch he steadied his horses and they went on driving down the road that led South as if they were both enveloped in a celestial light.

Chapter Seven

Vernita felt as if she had been driving forever.

There was no end to the countryside moving past her, the tall trees casting dark shadows on the narrow road and the sunshine which alternated with sharp showers of rain.

Fortunately, the Phaeton had a hood which kept her and Axel dry, and it was typical of the thoughtfulness of the De Cleremonts that Henri also had a small hood which he could pull over his perched-up seat behind.

The majority of aristocrats, Vernita realised, both in France and in England, did not take such care of their servants.

The out-riders fared worse, but they were tough men and seemed not to mind the rain beating in their faces or the wind threatening to blow their white wigs and velvet caps from their heads.

If the Inns were uncomfortable, Vernita hardly noticed it.

The years of privation had taken their toll of her strength and she found that not only did she sleep beside Axel in the Phaeton but she also fell asleep almost as soon as her head touched the pillow.

She hardly noticed whether the rooms in which they stayed were clean or dirty, or the food with which they were provided was good or bad.

"I am . . . sorry," she said to Axel as she realised

135

she had fallen asleep the night before while he was still kissing her.

"Do you suppose I do not understand?" he asked. "All I want, my precious, is to get you to England. Then you can rest and I will make you as you were meant to be at your age, glowing with health and happiness."

"I am glowing with happiness now," she replied. "I am more happy than I ever believed it was possible to be, because I love you so much."

"And I love you beyond words," he answered, holding her close against him.

Then once again they had to dress hurriedly and start off on the road which seemed to lead towards an ever-receding horizon which they would never reach.

Vernita ceased to notice the small towns through which they passed. Pouilly was known for its mineral waters, Nevers with its Cathedral and Ducal Palace, Moulins where Axel told her stood a memorial to the *Duc* de Montmorency, and finally Lyons, where two great rivers, the Saône and the Rhône, joined each other.

It had been a Roman city and there was, Vernita knew, a Roman theatre she would have loved to see, but she was too tired to do anything but want to sleep.

Actually it was a good thing she was not interested in the town, for the extremely narrow streets were badly paved and dirty and Axel told her that the women would have been very handsome had it not been for the fact that they were noted for losing their hair and their teeth when they were quite young.

"Why should that happen?" she asked.

"I am told the Doctors attribute it to the frequent fogs which cover the town," he replied, "but personally I think it has something to do with the bad water."

At Lyon they found a good Hotel—the Auberge

du Parc—where the food was certainly better than anything they had eaten before.

They had a comfortable Sitting-Room and Axel insisted as he had in other places where they stopped that Vernita did not change into one of the pretty evening-gowns that the *Vicomtesse* had given her.

Instead she put on a négligée which was as attractive as anything she had made for the Princess Paulina, and she reclined on the sofa while having her dinner.

A glass of champagne swept away much of her fatigue and while she and Axel laughed together she thought again and again that he was the most attractive man she had ever seen in her life.

When they had finished dinner the table was cleared away and he said to her:

"Now you must go to bed."

She held out her arms to him and whispered:

"Only if . . . you will . . . come too."

"You know that is what I want," he answered, "but I must see to the horses first, my darling. I was a little worried that the off-side leader seemed off-colour today."

Vernita looked apprehensive.

"Does that mean we will have to go slower?"

"Or buy another horse," Axel replied, "although I will never be able to purchase in a hurry anything half as good as those that Etienne has lent us."

He bent down and picked her up in his arms.

"I am going to carry you to bed," he said, "and let me tell you, you are far too light and I shall not be content until you need at least two men to carry you!"

She laughed at that, and putting her arm round his neck she drew his face down to hers.

"I am so afraid," she said, "that you will find this a very . . . boring honeymoon, since I do nothing but sleep. But I cannot tell you how much I love you."

"I am content for the moment to have a Sleeping Beauty for my wife," Axel answered, "and quite frankly, my darling, I drive better and quicker when you are not distracting me so that I want to kiss you."

He carried her into the adjacent room and laid her down on the bed.

"I shall not go to sleep until you return," Vernita said, "so please be very quick."

But she never knew if Axel hurried or not, for by the time he returned to her she was fast asleep and he did not wake her.

He stood beside the bed looking down at her by the light of the candles and there was a very tender expression on his face.

He knew how tired she must feel, for it was impossible to build up her strength in a few days after it had been drained away from her week after week, month after month, by lack of food and by constant anxiety.

He swore to himself as he looked at her lashes dark against her pale cheeks that he would make up to her for all she had suffered.

He knew that few women would have been so sweet and uncomplaining as she had been these last four days.

The roads had been rough, the showers of rain unpleasant, and some of the food they had been offered in the dirty Inns quite unpalatable.

But Vernita had only laughed at the unpleasantness of their surroundings.

When they had started off again in the Phaeton and she snuggled close to him to fall asleep almost immediately, he had driven on, loving her and knowing how fortunate he was in having a woman who could adjust herself to adversity.

There had been a great many women in Axel's life, which was not surprising considering how handsome he was. When he was a soldier in India and in his adventures in other countries he had not always travelled alone.

He had learnt to dread the type of woman who always wanted to draw attention to herself and who became sulky or petulant when things went wrong and never ceased complaining about what was unavoidable.

As Axel got into bed he resisted an impulse to draw Vernita to him and tell her how much he loved her.

Every day he felt that his love for her increased and certainly grew more passionate; but he loved her enough to be unselfish and know that sleep was what she needed as much as she needed to be fed.

He told himself that in the morning he would tell her how much he loved her, but, as it happened, when morning came there was no time.

They were awakened by Henri coming into the room soon after dawn.

Even as he crossed the darkened room towards the window to draw back the curtains, Axel was aware that something unusual had occurred, and he sat up in bed.

"What is it, Henri?" he asked.

The man came to the bed-side and said in a low voice:

"I did not disturb you last night, M'Lord, but there were two men, obviously members of the Police, asking questions of the landlord about his guests."

Axel's eyes were alert.

"Do you think they were suspicious of us?"

"I do not know, M'Lord, but they inspected the Phaeton where it was standing in the yard and asked one of the out-riders who was grooming the horses where you were going."

"He told them we were going to Nice?"

"Yes, that is what he said, M'Lord, but then they asked the landlord the same question and that seemed to me to be rather odd."

"We may be unnecessarily anxious," Axel said quietly, "but you know that Fouché has his spies everywhere. Although I think it unlikely that any of them have arrived here from Paris, ahead of us, we must take no chances."

"That is what I thought, M'Lord."

"Very well," Axel decided, "we will leave at once."

"I will see that the horses are ready, M'Lord."

Henri went from the room and Axel turned towards Vernita, who was only half-awake.

"What is ... it?" She yawned. "Surely it is too ... early for us to ... have to ... get up?"

"I am afraid we must leave immediately, my darling."

In an instant she was wide awake.

"What is wrong? What has happened?"

"Nothing to alarm you," Axel answered, "just a precaution against people who appear to be over-inquisitive. Hurry, my sweet!"

He kissed her lips, then as he moved from the bed she gave a little cry.

"Oh, Axel, I was asleep when you came back last night, and I tried so hard to keep awake!"

"You look very beautiful when you are asleep."

"But I missed talking to you."

"You missed more than that," he replied with a smile, "but we will make up for it once we get to England."

"Once we get to England!"

The words seemed to ring in Vernita's mind as she hurried into her clothes, feeling as if a cold hand clutched her heart and told her they were in danger.

Only when they were free of Lyons and once again out on the open road did she feel as if she could breathe again.

Now on the last part of their journey she found herself praying with an intensity greater than in any prayer she had said before that they would be able to escape to safety.

Even when she was asleep she dreamt that she still prayed and was still travelling on and on. . . .

Because she was so anxious and tired, the days seemed to draw out interminably and Vienne was only another Roman town which she was glad to leave because the next day brought them nearer to Marseilles.

They stayed the night at Valence and it seemed to Vernita more ominous than any other place at which they had stopped because Axel told her that it was where Napoleon had been educated when he was sixteen at the *École d'Artillerie*.

Even to think of the Emperor was to feel as if she were haunted by him and he was reaching out to make her his captive as he had done when he pulled her into his arms in the *Chambre de Parade*.

Only the timely interruption of Axel had prevented him from kissing her.

She had hated him then and she hated him even more now when she felt as if he was menacing her happiness and that after all they might not be able to escape him.

Soon Valence was left behind and they came to Montélimar, where France had grown her first almond tree in the sixteenth century, and their nougat, Axel told Vernita, was the most delicious in the world.

He bought her some and when they drove on the next day they ate it in the Phaeton and laughed over the sticky, delicious mess of it as if they were children.

The next night they reached Orange and as they drove through the Arc de Triomphe, which had been erected in 49 B.C. to celebrate a victory of Julius Caesar's, Vernita told herself that when they reached England they would erect their own Arc de Triomphe in gratitude for their triumphal escape.

It would not be a useless stone edifice, but if she and Axel could afford it they would build an Orphanage or endow a Hospital, anything that expressed their thankfulness and gratitude to God for having saved them.

For the first time she realised that the one thing she and Axel had never discussed was money.

She had taken it for granted that because he

looked rich he was rich, and the *Vicomtesse* had told her that his house was magnificent. But she knew no more and now she said to him as they drove along:

"We have never talked about it, but I suppose now that Papa is dead I inherit his estate in Buckinghamshire."

"Have I a wealthy wife as well as a beautiful one?" Axel asked.

"Is it important?" Vernita questioned.

"Not in the slightest," he answered, "I have sufficient for us both."

"You realise we have never talked about what we own?"

"There have been so many other more important things to say—when you are awake," he replied.

She blushed, then put her cheek against his arm.

"There will be lots to ... talk about when we have ... time."

"Many things," he agreed.

"We know so little about each other."

"I know everything that is important," he replied. "I know you are beautiful, sweet, kind, and clever. What else can one expect in one small person?"

Vernita thrilled at his words and the look in his eyes. Then she said:

"I only hope there is enough of ... me to keep you ... interested."

"You ought to last me for a few thousand years," he teased.

"But I would point out that I know little or nothing about you."

"You know that I love you and that should be enough to be going on with."

"The only thing that really matters is that you should love ... me," Vernita cried. "Oh, Axel, I am so terribly, crazily, wonderfully ... happy."

He laughed tenderly at the intensity with which she spoke. Then a little later she fell asleep beside him, a smile on her lips.

⟍ They drove into Marseilles when it was growing late in the evening and the streets were crowded not only with traffic but also with hundreds of people wandering about, apparently with nothing else to do.

Axel had difficulty in driving his Phaeton through them and they went through the town down towards the busy and prosperous port.

It was here that Vernita learnt for the first time they had to go into hiding until Axel could find a ship which would carry them along the coast to Gibraltar. The *Vicomte* had given him the name of a ship-owner whom he trusted.

The first thing they had to do when they arrived in Marseilles was to take leave of the Phaeton, the horses, and the out-riders.

It would have seemed strange for the *Vicomte* and *Vicomtesse* de Cleremont to be thinking of leaving France.

Accordingly, they stopped at a prosperous Inn ostensibly to enjoy a glass of wine, and Henri transferred their luggage from the Phaeton into a Hackney-carriage.

Then, after saying good-bye to the out-riders, one of whom took over the Phaeton, the other leading two horses, Axel and Vernita drove to a Lodging-House which, again, had been recommended by the *Vicomte*.

It was clean but simple. The owner did not even ask their names but showed them to a bed-room and Sitting-Room on the first floor from which they had a fine view of the port.

Henri, having unpacked what they would require and made up the bed, went downstairs to see what he could find them for supper.

"I am afraid this will not be very comfortable for you, my darling," Axel said apologetically.

"I assure you it is a Palace compared to the attic in which I lived with Mama for so long," Vernita replied.

"I keep forgetting when you look so elegant and so beautiful that you are used to roughing it." He smiled.

Vernita went nearer to him so that he could put his arms round her.

"It does not matter where I am as long as I am with . . . you," she said.

"That is what I want you to say," he answered. "At the same time, I want to give you every comfort in the world, surround you with luxury, and treat you like a Queen."

Vernita laughed.

"I have . . . everything I want at the . . . moment," she murmured, and drew a little closer to him.

He kissed her until the room swum dizzily round her and she felt as if they floated on clouds high up in the sky where they were alone and nothing else in the whole world mattered except themselves.

Then there was a knock on the door and Henri came in followed by a mob-capped maid carrying their supper.

It was a very simple meal but it was well-cooked and Axel admitted that the wine was at least drinkable.

Henri disappeared and Vernita was in bed before he returned when Axel spoke to him in the Sitting-Room.

"What have you discovered?" he asked.

"The ship belonging to Antoine Bouet is at sea, M'Lord, and nobody seems to know when it is likely to return," Henri replied.

"Then there is nothing we can do for the moment except stay here and hope that no-one becomes aware of it."

"That's what I thought, M'Lord," Henri agreed. "I'll go down to the port again tomorrow and hope it'll not be long before Bouet puts in an appearance."

"Did you find out anything else?" Axel enquired.

"Very little, M'Lord, except that the English have complete control of the Mediterranean and what French battle-ships there are in Marseilles are afraid to leave."

"Where is the main French Fleet?" Axel enquired.

"I'll try to ask some discreet questions tomorrow, M'Lord."

For the first time since they had left Paris, Vernita was able to sleep until late in the morning and Axel made no effort to wake her.

The sunshine came through the window, flooding the room with a golden light, and with Axel's arms round her, his lips and hands evoking sensations she had not known she was capable of feeling, Vernita had never been so happy.

Yet as the day passed she was aware that Axel was worried and when he stood at the window looking out at the ships in the port she knew without his telling her that he was apprehensive that if they had to wait too long for a ship, Fouché's Police might catch up with them.

Because she loved him and felt that she must do everything she could to alleviate his anxiety, she forced herself to appear gay and light-hearted and make him laugh.

When evening came he was increasingly restless and she knew that he was longing to go down to the port himself and see what he could discover.

Finally, when it was dark, as if he could bear it no longer, he told her that he must leave her for a short while and Vernita was terrified.

At the same time, she knew it was only because he loved her that Axel had stayed with her all day and allowed Henri to go alone to spy out the land.

With difficulty she bit back the protests which rose to her lips, merely saying in a voice which she strove to make sound normal:

"Do not be too ... long or you know I will fall ... asleep and regret bitterly that I was not ... waiting to ... greet my husband on his ... return."

Axel put his arms round her and turned her face up to his.

He looked into her eyes and was well aware what she was feeling and the effort she was making on his behalf.

"You are perfect in every possible way," he said.

"Do not worry, my precious, we shall not lose each other now."

He kissed her passionately, then he was gone, and Vernita clenched her hands together to prevent herself from screaming.

It was an agony that seemed to sear its way into her very soul as she sat alone hour after hour, thinking in her anxiety that each minute that passed seemed like a century.

Supposing Axel never returned? Supposing he was caught and imprisoned and she never knew what had happened to him?

Then she told herself that God and her mother, who had looked after her until now, were still there to support and protect her and she was not really alone.

She thought of sleeping but that was impossible.

Instead she walked about the room watching the stars come out in the sky and the lights from the ships reflected on the water of the harbour.

What was Axel doing? Who was he talking to? Why had he stayed away for so long?

At last she heard footsteps on the stairs and when the door opened and he stood there she gave a cry that seemed to echo round the walls and ran towards him.

He caught her in his arms and she clung to him, speechless with relief, yet still trembling from the ordeal through which she had passed.

"I thought you would be asleep, my darling," he exclaimed.

Then as he saw her pale cheeks and the fear which still lingered in her eyes, he said:

"You should have trusted me, but I did not mean to upset you, my precious."

He kissed her; then, realising she was cold, he carried her in his arms to a sofa and sat down holding her against his heart as if she were a child who needed comforting.

Vernita hid her face against his neck and he kissed her forehead and her hair and one small ear before he said:

"I have good news, my darling."

"Good news?"

"Yes, Bouet's ship came in tonight. That is why I was so long. I have spoken to him and we leave at dawn tomorrow!"

"For Gibraltar?"

"I have a better idea."

"What is that?"

"Bouet has learnt that Lord Nelson, who as you know is the British Commander-in-Chief in the Mediterranean, has left the Scillies and is sailing this way. We will try to intercept him."

"Intercept Lord Nelson?" Vernita questioned. "But where is he taking the British Fleet?"

"There is a rumour, Bouet told me, that the French ships, which have been joined by the Spanish are sailing towards the West Indies. If that is so, Nelson will follow them."

"And what will happen to . . . us?"

Axel smiled.

"If I can once get you aboard a British Man-o'-War, my darling, then I do not care where we go. All I know is that we shall be safe, and the French Fleet, wherever Nelson meets them, will be annihilated as they were at the Battle of the Nile."

It sounded rather dangerous to Vernita to be in the middle of a sea-battle.

But at the moment it was difficult to think of anything but that Axel's arms were round her, he was with her again, and at least for the next few hours she need not be afraid.

Again they passed a very short night.

When the streets were still dark and practically empty except for a few scavengers, they crept down to the port. Henri was carrying their luggage, assisted by the tired and somewhat taciturn owner of the boarding house.

He however cheered up when Axel rewarded him with an unprecedented number of gold pieces and he wished them *Bon Voyage* with an unmistakable note of sincerity in his voice.

The ship owned by Antoine Bouet, who Vernita was to learn later had carried quite a number of refugees sent him by the *Vicomte* de Cleremont, was to her relief larger than she had expected.

It was ostensibly a fishing vessel, but its owner was, although he took great risks, making very much more money by carrying human cargo than he would ever have done by letting down his nets.

He was a hearty, tough, sea-faring man who informed Axel that he had no use for politics and all he asked was to be left alone by Government Officials and allowed to get on with his own business.

"Always interfering, always nosing into an honest man's private affairs!" he grumbled. "They're nothing more than parasites and we who work have to keep 'em!"

He spoke for a great number of Frenchmen who, while they were prepared to air their views to strangers, were usually far too frightened to speak so frankly except in the privacy of their own homes.

Antoine Bouet took his ship out of port on the early morning tide and only as they reached the open sea and no-one had seemed concerned with their leaving did Vernita give a deep sigh of relief.

As she stood on deck Axel put his arm round her and she knew by the expression on his face that he was feeling as if a great burden had fallen from his shoulders.

"We have escaped!" she said in a low voice.

"Not quite," he replied. "We still have to be watchful in case we encounter one of the Barbary Pirates or a French frigate which could ask why we are so far from the fishing grounds."

He spoke warningly but the light in his eyes belied his own caution.

Then he said, his arms tightening round her:

"What we have to look out for now is the British Fleet."

"You are . . . sure they are . . . somewhere in the . . . Mediterranean?"

"It is not only what I have heard but what I feel

in my bones," Axel replied. "If it is true that the French and Spanish ships have sailed for the West Indies, Nelson will follow them."

Unfortunately, the weather, which had seemed fair when they left port, worsened.

There were blustery winds and sharp squalls, and Vernita was thankful that although it was extremely uncomfortable and the constant changes of tack was very wearying she did not feel sea-sick.

Axel however insisted that she should lie down in the cabin for fear that she might be thrown about and hurt herself.

She was glad to obey him and while he went on deck because she knew he wanted to watch for the British ships, she slept or awoke to pray a prayer of gratitude that every hour they were at sea took them farther and farther away from France.

Two days of pitching and tossing, with at times the waves breaking over the small ship, were very tiring.

It was only after they had spent two nights aboard and part of the third day that Vernita heard a great shout go up from the deck above her and Axel came hurrying down the companionway into the cabin.

There was no need for him to say they had sighted the British Fleet—the expression on his face would have told her what had happened even if she had not heard the crew cheering.

He kissed her, then even as she clung to him he went up on deck again.

She followed him a few minutes later after putting on the warm velvet cloak trimmed with sable the *Vicomtesse* had given her.

Looking from the deck towards the horizon, she saw a marvellous sight: two three-deckers and twenty-three battle-cruisers with every sail full-bellied tacking against the wind.

It was so impressive, so beautiful, that she felt her heart swell with pride and she knew Axel felt the same.

Bouet had been sailing his ship for the last two days without flying a flag, but now on Axel's instructions he ran up the Union Jack and the flag of distress.

Because of the veering wind it took them some time to reach the ships. Then almost quicker than Vernita could hope for she was being helped up a rope-ladder to the Flagship which Axel told her belonged to the Admiral.

She paused when she reached the deck to wave her hand to the seamen who had brought them to safety, then they were being taken to the Admiral's cabin and for the first time in her life Vernita met Lord Nelson.

She was astonished to find he was an even smaller man than she had expected, and the fact that he had only one arm and a patch over one eye made him look strange.

At the same time, she was perceptive enough to realise that here in a small body was a very great man.

Power and authority emanated from him even as it had seemed to emanate from Axel, and when as she curtseyed he smiled, she understood why Lady Hamilton found him irresistible.

"My name is Tregarron, My Lord Admiral," she heard Axel say, "and my wife and I are escaping from Napoleon's Police."

"I have heard of you, My Lord," Lord Nelson replied. "In fact the Prime Minister was speaking of you when I was last in England."

"I have no need to repeat the compliment where you are concerned, My Lord Admiral." Axel smiled.

They sat down and told Lord Nelson of their adventures. Only when he had heard how they had escaped and had commended Axel on the information he had acquired in Paris did he tell them of his own troubles.

"Admiral Villeneuve avoided my lookout off Cape Sebastian," he said, "and is on his way West, not East as had been expected. I am trying to make up for the muddle the Government has made in not informing me what was occurring, but the wind has been dead in my teeth."

"It has been very rough for the last two days," Axel said.

"In nine days I have covered only two hundred miles," Lord Nelson groaned. "My fortune seems to have flown away."

"Do you think you will have missed the French?" Axel enquired.

"I hope God will be merciful, but a passing merchantman told me that the French have been seen off the Spanish Coast sailing West."

"And you think you can overtake them?" Axel questioned.

"I can only try," Lord Nelson replied. "I have had to leave five of my frigates to guard the two Scillies, and only today have I made any progress against the sailor's worst enemy—the weather!"

They talked for a little longer, then Lord Nelson informed them that when they reached Gibraltar if the weather was fair he intended to stay for only a few hours.

"You will go West, My Lord?" Axel asked.

"I shall make for Madeira and then West," Lord Nelson replied. "If I fail to find the French, if they have not gone to the West Indies, I shall be blamed; to be burned in effigy or Westminster Abbey is my alternative."

Axel was silent and Vernita knew he was tense.

Lord Nelson must have known what he was feeling, because he smiled.

"As far as you are concerned, you need not worry, My Lord. I must send a ship back to England to report where I am going and where I expect to find the French. You and your wife can travel in her."

"Thank you, My Lord Admiral," Axel replied.

There was a note of relief and sincerity in his voice that was unmistakable.

They were shown into a cabin that they could occupy until they reached Gibraltar.

It was not as large as Lord Nelson's but it was comfortable enough, and for the moment nothing mattered except that the nightmare was over, the fear had vanished, and they were together.

As the door shut behind them Axel held out his arms and Vernita threw herself against him.

He undid the ribbons of her bonnet and lifted it from her head. Then as the ship lurched he picked her up in his arms and laid her on the bed.

She lay against the pillows, looking up at him with a smile, and he pulled off his tight-fitting coat, then sat on the mattress, facing her.

"It is all over, my darling," he said. "We have escaped!"

"We have . . . escaped!" she repeated with a little sob in her voice because it seemed so poignant.

"We have escaped from France and Napoleon," Axel said, "but there is one thing from which we cannot ever escape."

"What is that?" she asked apprehensively.

"From love," he answered. "The love I have for you, my dearest heart, that will keep you my prisoner now and forever. You will never escape me!"

Vernita laughed.

"Do you think I would want to?"

Then looking into Axel's eyes she put her arms round his neck and drew him down until his lips were very near to hers.

"I want to be your . . . prisoner. I want you to . . . hold me and . . . keep me not only in your . . . arms but in your . . . heart for the rest of our lives . . . together."

"You are in my heart," Axel replied, "and you are a part of me so that I cannot live without you."

Her arms were drawing his head still closer but for a moment he resisted her.

"You have been so brave, so wonderful, my lovely wife," he said. "Now I can give you everything you want, everything you deserve."

"That is . . . easy," Vernita whispered, "I want only . . . you."

"I am yours, as you are mine," Axel said.

Then as if he could resist her no longer his lips came down on hers.

She thrilled to the fire of them and the passion which made him hold her so tightly against his heart that she could feel it beating frantically against hers.

"I love ... you ... love me ... Oh, Axel, love me!" she wanted to say.

But it was impossible to speak.

She could only feel the glory and wonder of his love enveloping her and arousing something wild and fiery within them both.

It made them oblivious of everything but their need for each other as the sails billowing out overhead carried them towards England and home.